THE CASE OF
MISTAKEN
IDENTITY

a mac & sam
mystery

A NOVEL BY

DEBORAH SPRINKLE

Scrivenings
PRESS
Quench your thirst for story.
www.ScriveningsPress.com

Published by Scrivenings Press LLC
15 Lucky Lane
Morrilton, Arkansas 72110
https://ScriveningsPress.com

Printed in the United States of America

Paperback ISBN 978-1-64917-309-6

eBook ISBN 978-1-64917-310-2

Editors: Erin R. Howard and Heidi Glick

Cover design by Linda Fulkerson
www.bookmarketinggraphics.com
Cover background photo by Deborah Sprinkle.

All characters are fictional, and any resemblance to real people, either factual or historical, is purely coincidental.

PRAISE FOR DEBORAH SPRINKLE

The Case of Mistaken Identity is a suspenseful novel with a romantic thread guaranteed to keep readers turning the pages as the dangers of mistaken identity threaten lives. A great read. Don't miss it.

— LORETTA EIDSON, *AWARD-WINNING* AUTHOR

The Case of Mistaken Identity is another great mystery from Deborah Sprinkle that will have you flipping the pages to find the murderer!

— PATRICIA BRADLEY, USA BEST-SELLING ROMANTIC SUSPENSE AUTHOR OF *COUNTER ATTACK, BOOK 1 IN THE PEARL RIVER SERIES*

A recommended read! Sharing the looks of a beautiful woman can be fun—unless it's murder.

— DIANN MILLS, AUTHOR OF *FACING THE ENEMY*—TYNDALE DIANNMILLS.COM

To my husband, Les.

Acknowledgments

Let me begin with my loyal readers—those of you who continue to ask when my next book is coming out, share my books with your friends and family, and write such wonderful reviews. You are blessings beyond words in my life!

To my Word Weaver posse, Bonnie Sue Beardsley, Starr Ayers, Denise Holmberg, Linda Dindzans, Caroline Powers, Sandra Vosburgh, and Sandra Melville Hart. You are amazing! Your encouragement and support keeps me striving to be a better writer and a better person.

For Detective Lieutenant Steve Sitzes of the Washington Police Department—he got a promotion since my first book—I will say it again. I can't thank you enough for sharing your expertise with me and helping to make this book as true to life as possible. I take full responsibility for any mistakes in procedure, etc.

For DiAnn Mills, my mentor and my friend. Thank you for always being on the other end of the phone when I need you.

And for Patricia Bradley, my friend, encourager, and another source of wisdom, thank you.

If you get the idea that a lot of help was needed in writing this book, you'd be correct. I strive to make each of my books the best it can be. None of them is perfect, but my hope is that each one is better than the ones before. Writing is a journey and a journey is best made with friends.

Along with all the wonderful people I've already

mentioned, I have found a second family in Scrivenings Press with Linda Fulkerson. She has created not only an excellent publishing house, but a family of authors who lift each other up, full of support and love. I thank God He directed my books to you, Linda.

Last, but not least, I want to mention my biggest fan, the man who completes me, my husband of over 50 years, Les Sprinkle. He prepares the way for me to write by taking care of most everything to do with the house, and takes care of me too. I thank God every day for him

CHAPTER 1

In the brisk November wind, the helium balloons pulled and twisted against her grasp like rebellious toddlers. Private Investigator Mackenzie Love threw an ugly look at the shiny bags of gas and tightened her grip. Mama always said patience was a learned virtue. In that case, she still had a lot to learn.

She hurried across the lot to where she'd parked her new four-door sedan well away from the other vehicles. As usual, it no longer stood by itself. Pickups, vans, and SUVs hemmed it in on three sides and formed an island of metal in a sea of asphalt. What was wrong with people?

At the car, the real battle began. Mac opened the rear door and wrestled her charges into the backseat. By the time she'd safely tucked the last balloon inside, sweat trickled down her neck. She withdrew from the car and slammed the door.

Her partner, Samantha Majors, should have done balloon duty. After all, she drove an SUV. But Sam was busy this morning getting ready for her mother's visit.

An itching sensation traveled the back of Mac's neck. She lifted a hand to scratch as a low voice sounded behind her.

"Too bad you won't get to enjoy those."

Mac pivoted, ready for a fight. "Back off. I'm in no mood for jokes."

Her words faded away, and beads of sweat turned to ice water. The barrel of a gun filled her vision—pointed straight at her heart.

"You have been hard to find. Come with us like a good girl."

Mac tore her eyes away from the pistol and took a mental mug shot for later—if there was a later.

"Who are you?" She fought to keep her voice from shaking.

Lines of confusion flashed across the man's brow. And he made a fatal error—he shifted his weight to his back foot and took his focus off his gun for an instant. But an instant was all Mac needed.

Adrenaline surged through her as she lunged forward and snapped her left forearm under his gun hand. The spit of a suppressed weapon sounded next to her ear, but her assailant managed to hold on to his pistol. Mac wasn't out of danger yet.

With her other hand, she delivered a lightning punch to the man's ribs. He bent at the waist and wrapped his arms around his stomach.

"Hey." A parking lot guard appeared out of nowhere. "What's going on here?"

Distracted, Mackenzie glanced toward the approaching man. The last thing she wanted was someone else hurt. "Stay back." She waved him away.

"You witch." Her attacker swung his gun arm in an arc and caught Mac next to her right eye with the hard metal of his weapon.

Fireworks exploded in her head. She fumbled for a hold and prayed she'd stay conscious.

Behind Mackenzie's car, a white van screeched to a halt, and the man jumped inside.

The adrenaline release left Mac shaken. She opened her car door and slid into the driver's seat.

"Are you all right?" The guard peered at her. "I've called 911."

"I'm fine." Mac jerked her head at the retreating van. "Get the license plate."

The guard rushed into the open parking lot.

Mac laid her forehead on the steering wheel and groaned. How had a simple trip to get balloons turned into a man pointing a gun at her and a 911 call?

"Sorry, miss. The van didn't have a plate." The guard reached a hand in her direction. "There's blood running down your face."

"Figures." Mac dabbed her head with a tissue and winced.

An ambulance pulled in behind her car, and an EMT trotted over.

"Could you turn to face me, ma'am?"

Ma'am? Things were going from bad to worse.

The medical technician cleaned the wound. "Could use a stitch or two. Want me to do it here or go to the hospital?"

"Here." It would take a lot more than a cut on the head to get her into the hospital again. Like maybe a severed ear, or a leg.

The EMT returned with equipment from his truck and sewed her up. Two stitches and a gauze dressing later, he pronounced her ready to go.

"Thanks." Mac explored the bandage on her face with her fingers.

"Hi, Mackenzie." Washington, Missouri, Detective Victor Young strode over to her. "Before you leave, I need a statement."

"I've got a splitting headache, Vic. Can we do this later?"

"You know it's better while it's fresh."

She nodded and cringed as a sharp pain stabbed her temple. "I was so busy putting those dumb balloons in the car, I didn't realize the man was behind me until he spoke."

Detective Young's eyes narrowed as he listened to her story.

"I don't know who the man was or who he thought I was." The memory of the gun sent a chill down her spine. Mac rubbed her arms.

She'd had guns pointed at her before, but she'd expected it—been prepared. This guy came out of nowhere. She vowed to never let it happen again.

"You must have a doppelgänger."

"A what?"

"A twin—someone who looks like you. In your case, someone in a lot of trouble." A crease appeared on Detective Young's brow. "You'll need to come to the station and help with a sketch."

"I'd like to get these balloons out of my car." Mac glanced at her backseat. "And get something for my headache."

"The balloons will be fine, and I've got aspirin at the precinct." Young closed his notebook. "I'll see you at the station."

Mac cast a scowl toward Detective Young's retreating back, retrieved her phone, and pressed two.

"Mackenzie Love and Samantha Majors, Private Investigators. How can we help you?"

"Hi, Sam." Mac started her car, and the phone switched to her radio speakers.

"Hi, yourself. Did you get the balloons?"

"Yep."

"What happened, Mac?"

"I haven't said three words." Mac raised an eyebrow at her phone. "What makes you think something happened?"

"Because you only said three words. By now, I'd be getting an earful about how you'll never volunteer to get the balloons for anything ever again."

"Sam, sometimes you scare me. I'm on my way to the police station."

"Hang on. I'm putting you on speaker so Miss P can hear this."

Mac gave her partner and their researcher/secretary, Miss Prudence Freebody, the short version of her attack. "Now I've got to help the police with a sketch, and my head's pounding."

"I'll meet you at the station," Sam said. "For moral support, and I'll bring ibuprofen."

"Thanks. I can use both." Mac ended the call and pulled her seat belt across her torso. She wasn't excited about a visit to the police station. Not because she wasn't welcome there, but because Detective Jake Sanders, Sam's brother, worked there.

Mac's pulse raced. She and Jake dated—sort of. A family emergency interrupted their one and only date, and since then, he'd been in Florida for a month. But the brief time they'd spent together left her with memories of his embrace, his kiss, and murmured words of love. They'd filled her dreams while he was gone.

Mac hadn't seen him since he'd returned to Washington. She touched a finger to her lips. Would their first meeting be awkward? Would he regret asking her out?

And there was Nate, Miss P's nephew, and her college boyfriend. Why did he have to set up his law practice in Washington? Mac groaned. Maybe she should give up dating altogether.

CHAPTER 2

Mac surveyed the entrance to the Public Safety building, home of the Washington police force. She half expected Jake to be waiting for her at the door. But he wasn't there, and a twinge of disappointment shot through her.

Sam pulled in next to her. "Ready to rock and roll?" She hitched her shoulder bag in place and smiled at Mac.

"I guess. This is not how I planned to spend my day."

"I know." She gave Mac a little shove. "Let's get it over with, and we can get back to preparing for our party."

Inside, they climbed the steps to the second floor, where the police precinct was located. The woman behind the counter gave them a broad smile.

"Hello, you two. Haven't seen you in a while." She picked up the receiver to her phone. "Here to see your brother, Detective Sanders?"

"It's Detective Young this time," Mac said. "I'm here to work with someone on a sketch."

"So, you're the one." She punched a button. "Mackenzie

Love is here." She hung up and faced them. "He'll be right with you. That must have been scary today. How are you, Miss Love?"

"A little headache, but I'll live." Mac gave her a wry smile and turned as Detective Young approached.

"Hi, ladies." He motioned them to follow. "Let's go back to my desk. Detective Walker's waiting for you there." He led them through the maze of cubbyholes to a small office in the rear.

A man with brown skin and warm brown eyes stood as they entered the room.

"Detective Walker, this is Mackenzie Love and her partner, Samantha Majors. They're private investigators." Young nodded at Sam. "Jake Sanders is Sam's brother."

"I've heard about you two." Walker's natural smile put Mac at ease. "Why don't you ladies have a seat, and we'll get started." He sat behind a computer and punched a few keys. "Let's begin with what the gunman was wearing."

"Worn jeans and a long-sleeve dark T-shirt. I couldn't tell if it was black or navy blue," Mackenzie said.

"Any writing on it or an insignia?"

"Nothing that stood out."

"Good." He entered the information and smiled at Mac. "Now let's talk about his face."

Mackenzie closed her eyes. An image of the gun filled her mind as she tried to recall the details of her attack.

"Are you all right?" Sam touched her arm. "You moaned."

"I'm okay." Mac gave her a brief smile and closed her eyes again. On the screen of her mind, she lifted her eyes once more. "He had dark skin, but he seemed ... European, if that makes any sense. With a narrow chin."

"Italian or Spanish?"

"Possible."

"Could you tell if his face was oval? Square? Round?"

She pinched her brows together. "Square. I think."

"Any facial hair?"

Was there a mustache? She pressed her hands to her temples. "No, nothing."

"Okay. What about his other features?"

"His nose was sharp, and he had thin lips."

Keys clicked as Walker entered the new information. "How about his eyes?"

"He wore dark glasses. Small ones." The man's face came into focus in her mind. "And a navy ball cap." Her eyes popped open. "And a short scar on his left cheekbone."

"Great." Walker moved his mouse over an area of his screen. "The hat means he could be bald or have a full head of hair, but no problem."

"I guess so." A sudden weariness came over her. She opened her eyes. It didn't sound like much to go on.

"Give me a moment, and I'll have a sketch for you to look at." Walker bent close to the screen. "Here it is." He swiveled the computer around for Mac to see. "What do you think?"

The image of her attacker jerked her out of her stupor. "You did it."

"Don't sound so surprised." Walker chuckled. "I've been doing this for a long time, and you gave me great details." He pivoted the computer back to face him. "I'll finish putting the information with this, and by afternoon, it'll be out to every police station in the area. We'll get him."

"Get who?" Detective Jake Sanders strolled into the room. "Hi, Sis. Mackenzie."

He brushed Mac's shoulder as he passed, and for a moment, she lost track of where she was.

Detective Walker nodded his head at the computer screen. "This is the guy who attacked Mackenzie this morning."

"I didn't hear about the attack." Jake tensed. "What happened?"

"Mackenzie was leaving the store when this guy with a gun ambushed her. She fought him off, but he hit her in the head and got away."

Jake's blue eyes darkened as he took in the bandage near Mac's right eye. She winced inwardly under his intense gaze. It wasn't the first time she'd gotten smacked on the head, but as she and Jake grew closer, he seemed more agitated each time it happened.

"It's not as bad as it seems." She straightened and stared back, hoping to deflect a future lecture.

"Hmm." He returned his attention to the sketch. "I assume this will go out to all the surrounding local law enforcement?"

"Already working on it," Walker said.

"Great." Jake gave the women a grim smile. "I'll see you two later."

Mac waited for him to touch her shoulder again on his way out, but he didn't. A kernel of regret lodged in her throat.

"Thanks for coming in." Detective Walker stood. "If we think of any more questions, we'll be in touch."

"Our pleasure." Sam steered Mac out of the room and to the parking lot. "Let's get back to the office and help Ms. P with the party."

Mac pulled her sunglasses from her purse. If asked to list the top five things she preferred doing right now, throwing a party would rank minus ten—along with cleaning the bathroom. Especially after seeing Jake.

Saturday night, Mac and Sam planned to celebrate five years in business. They'd invited everyone—past clients, friends, and family.

Which meant Miss Priscilla Freebody, their associate, and her nephew, Nathanial Xander Westcott III, former boyfriend to Mackenzie. And the other reason she'd avoided Jake. He didn't know about Nate. She hadn't even told Sam.

Detective Jake Sanders slammed his door, slumped in his chair, and cast an angry look over the files piled on his desk. Nothing had changed since he'd been away. Mac landed in the middle of trouble on a simple shopping trip. Didn't he have enough to deal with in his job without having to worry about her, too?

He punched the side of his file cabinet. Pain shot up his arm. Dumb move. The photo on top fell over. He picked it up.

With a big smile on her face, Mackenzie stood next to his sister in front of the house they used for their offices. Mac's dark hair blew in the breeze, and her chestnut eyes gleamed as if picturing future adventures. A thundercloud passed across his brow. Why did he want to yell at her and kiss her at the same time? Maybe dating her was a big mistake.

He swiveled his chair toward his desk and his backlog of paperwork. Besides, he didn't have time to go out. And after seeing the pain his mom suffered through this past month with his dad, he wasn't certain he wanted to get close to anyone. A simple life of work and friends sounded pretty good about now.

CHAPTER 3

As Mac neared the small house at the corner of Second and Johnson, it was all she could do not to turn around and run the other way. She glanced in the mirror at the shiny bags of helium, and frustration turned her stomach.

The little monsters wouldn't get a chance to fly away at this point. Not when she'd gotten them this far. Mac closed the front door to her car before opening the back one.

Sam pulled into the driveway behind her.

"Freedom is not an option." Mac gave the helium balloons her sternest look and transferred them from the backseat to her tightfisted grip.

Sam came behind her. "They're beautiful."

"I guess." Mac peered at them.

"Before we go in, I should let you know Miss P told me about Nate."

Mac's stomach churned. "What did she say?"

"That you dated him in college and have been helping him get settled in Washington," Sam said. "Why didn't you tell me yourself?"

"I don't know. I guess because Jake's your brother, and ..."

"I told you before, all I care about is that you and my brother are happy, whether it's together or with someone else."

"Well, I'm pretty sure Jake and I aren't together anymore—at least not as far as he's concerned."

"What makes you say that?" Sam pushed her hair behind an ear.

"I could tell. He's upset because I didn't call him when the guy attacked me and because I've got another bump on the head. He's probably rethinking getting involved with me."

"Mac, you're crazy. You can't help it if you get hit on the head. He's upset with himself because he can't keep you safe. Men are protective. It's their nature."

"Is Alan like that?" Mac shrugged her purse on her shoulder.

Sam laughed. "He gets mad if I get a splinter."

"Yeah, well, let's see how Jake feels after he meets Nate." Mac opened the door to their offices. "Miss P, we're back." She maneuvered the balloons inside and pulled up short.

"Mac, let me in." Sam pushed her to one side and let out a low whistle.

Twenty latex balloons in all the colors of the rainbow floated around the room. Where had they come from?

"Aren't they marvelous?" Miss P waved her hand in the air and set the bright orbs into motion. "Nate bought them for us. I do believe it makes the place more festive." Miss P took the shiny helium balloons from Mac and tied weights to the ends of their strings. "Oh my, these are perfect."

It was then Mac noticed him standing a few feet to her left. Nathaniel Xander Westcott III. His smoky gray eyes held their usual gleam, which always made her feel guilty—as if they shared a secret. Did he look at all women like that, or only her?

"I don't believe we've met." Sam held out her hand. "I'm Samantha Majors."

Nate shifted his gaze to Sam, and a grin sprang across his face. "I'm glad we finally meet. My aunt has told me so much about you."

"I know a lot about you as well." Sam disengaged her hand from his. "Thanks for helping with our party."

"My pleasure. Mac and I go way back. Did she tell you we dated in college?"

His warm voice washed over Mac, and her pulse ratcheted. She flashed a pleading look at her friend and partner.

Sam nodded and pulled Mac farther into the room. "Let's see what's left to be done."

"Thanks," she whispered.

"You're welcome," Sam murmured loud enough for her to hear.

"The table looks great." Mac smoothed a wrinkle on the white tablecloth. "It's all ready for the food." She scanned the area. "And I like the way you placed the chairs."

"That was Nate's idea." Miss P beamed at her nephew. "He felt it would be best to put them in sets of two or three, with a small table near each grouping."

"Good idea." Samantha flashed a smile at him. "What else needs to be done?"

Miss P surveyed the room. "I'll dust and run the vacuum one more time Saturday morning, but I don't see much else. A few last-minute details may arise."

"Okay." Sam clapped her hands. "Mac, you and I have work to do." She shot Mac a work-with-me-here look.

"Yes." *Sam to the rescue again.* "If you'll excuse us, we'll be in our offices. Knock if you need anything." She hurried across the floor.

"May I speak to you a moment?" Nate stepped between Mac and her office door.

Mac's heart skipped a beat. She pressed her lips together in frustration at her lack of control.

"But if you don't have time ..." Nate retreated a step.

"No, no. My head is hurting." She forced a smile. "Come in. It's time for more pain medicine."

"Which brings me to what I want to talk to you about." He followed her into her office and sat down. "I'm offering you my services as your attorney for free."

"Why would I need an attorney?" Had the bump on her head addled her brain?

"When the police find this guy—"

"Nate, we have prosecutors for that."

"I know." He rolled his eyes. "But you hit the guy, right? He might decide to sue, and if he does, I want to defend you."

Mac's mouth dropped open. Was that even a possibility? "Sue *me?*"

"Yes." Nate placed his elbows on his knees and clasped his hands together. "It happens all the time."

Mac studied him for a moment. "Nate, I appreciate your concern for me, but I'll deal with being sued if it happens." She pushed away from her desk. "Thanks for the offer."

Nate stood. "You're welcome." The corners of his mouth lifted in a cockeyed grin. "Just taking care of old friends. I'll let you get back to work." He sauntered out the door.

Mac collapsed into her chair. Why were her times with Nate so emotionally exhausting? Just because they had a thing in college didn't mean she still cared for him in a romantic way. Did it?

Mackenzie pulled a photo from her top drawer. A girl with long hair lounged in the arms of a boy with a beard, mustache, and hair almost as long as the girl's. They smiled at the camera as if they didn't have a care in the world.

What they had wasn't love, but they'd been close, and for a time, after she'd graduated, she missed having Nate in her life. He seemed different now—beyond short hair and being clean shaven. He was more self-assured.

In college, despite his looks, Nate was kind and respectful, and she felt safe with him. She glanced at her door. This version of her former boyfriend still had those same traits, but he wasn't a boy any longer. He was a man. And she responded to him as a woman does to a man, whether she wanted to or not.

Miss P stuck her head in the door. "Mr. Fischer's on the line."

"I'll take it in Sam's office." Mac got there as the phone rang. "Mr. Fischer? Hang on. I'm putting you on speaker." She glanced at Sam. "How can we help you?"

"I have a curious problem and could use your expertise."

"What is it?" Sam asked.

"It's hard to explain. Would you be available to meet?"

Sam tapped some keys on her computer and brought up their calendar.

"When did you have in mind?"

"I've got back-to-back meetings tomorrow, and you have your party on Saturday. How is Sunday afternoon for you?"

Mac squinted at the computer screen. "Two o'clock?"

"Good." He paused. "By the way, I may not make it to your party. I'll explain on Sunday."

CHAPTER 4

Sleep had eluded Sam. She put it down to Mac being attacked, the strange call from Mr. Fischer, and general anxiety about the party. The trees she and Alan planted last year cast long shadows in the early morning sun. With every gust of wind, more leaves took flight. Soon the limbs would be bare. She sipped her coffee as she gazed out the kitchen window.

Exercise and fresh air should get her juices flowing. She rinsed her cup and turned. "Killer? Want to go for a walk?"

A champagne-colored golden doodle bounced into the kitchen, tongue hanging out and tail swishing back and forth. Sam stooped and rubbed the dog's head.

"Look out, cats and squirrels, here we come." She fitted him with a harness and clipped on a leash. "I think we'll go into the woods."

The small forest behind their property sold Sam and Alan on the house. When they put up the fence, they installed a gate in the back to provide access. It was Sam's favorite place for walks.

Killer's tail launched into overdrive as soon as they left through the back door. Sam chuckled. Her puppy enjoyed the woods too. More squirrels.

At the gate, she tugged on his leash. "Sit."

He sat and turned mournful eyes on her.

"You know the drill." She raised an eyebrow. "I go through first."

On the other side of the gate, she allowed Killer to lead. As she followed him into the coolness of the woods, peace settled over her. She drew in a deep breath.

The earthy smell of wood, moss, new life, and decay blended to open her lungs. Filtered sunlight created a warm play of color and shadows while the muted calls of birds provided background music.

Sam lost track of time and allowed her dog to guide her deeper into the trees. Killer surged forward and yanked her off balance. After a few staggering steps, she dug her heels in.

"Stop." She hauled back on the leash with both hands.

He sat, head lowered, and eyes focused on the trail ahead.

"What is wrong with you?" She squatted next to him and placed a hand on his head. His body trembled. Killer stared down the trail and whimpered.

She peeked at her watch. "No time to explore, buddy. We need to head home." She tugged on Killer's leash. "We'll come back another day."

Once she turned him toward home, Sam didn't have to tell him twice. Killer pulled like a sled dog in the traces. When they reached the gate, Sam took off his leash to let him run around the yard, but he made a beeline for the back door.

"What's with you today?" She grabbed his head and pushed the hair away from his eyes. They seemed moist and clear. He licked her mouth, and she sputtered. "Thanks for that, dog."

In the house, he headed for his water dish while Sam wiped her face. She cut a look at the clock on the wall. In about twenty-four hours, her mom would be here from Florida. When Sam told her about the anniversary party, she insisted on coming.

The house was ready for her visit, but was Sam? It would be the first time her mom traveled anywhere since her dad was admitted to the Alzheimer's care home and the first time Sam had been with her mom without her dad in a long time. She touched the glass cross hanging in the window. Rainbows of light danced on the kitchen counter.

Lord, bless our time together.

Killer pawed the door to the refrigerator and gave her one of his most pitiful looks.

"You want an ice cube?" She opened the freezer drawer and pushed her dog's head away. "You know better." Using a scoop, she retrieved two ice cubes and tossed them on the floor.

Killer grabbed one and tossed it in the air.

"Have fun, you silly boy. I have to get ready for work."

But when she left the kitchen, he abandoned his play and followed her back to the bedroom. As she prepared to leave, Killer stuck to her side with every step.

She bent and lifted his face to hers. "I'll be back soon. You'll be okay."

He sat and offered her his paw.

"I promise." She shook his soft foot and left.

"TELL me you're on your way." Mackenzie fought to keep her voice calm without success. "I'm having a real problem with Nate." She peeked through the crack in her door. "He helps me with every little thing and reminisces about our time in college."

"You poor thing. A handsome, intelligent man who adores you and is at your beck and call. How do you cope?"

"It's not funny, Sam. I don't want another man in my life." Desperation seeped into her tone. "I'm trying to date your brother, remember?"

"How is it you're brave enough to tackle a man with a gun but have so much trouble handling your love life?" Sam chuckled.

"Oh sure, laugh. You're not the one who—" Voices sounded in the living room. "Miss P and Nate are back from the store. Get here fast," Mac hissed into the phone.

She pressed End and closed her door. For a long moment, her fingers played with the lock, but she resisted the temptation and walked back to her desk.

"There you are." Nate pushed her door open. "Ready for lunch? We brought back burgers."

Mac sighed. "Sure."

"We'll eat in here since the table's ready for the party."

Mac closed her computer and shuffled her papers before plopping them on the floor beside her. Another thing she'd have to do before tomorrow afternoon. Find a place for her mess.

Nate dragged two chairs in and put three placemats on Mac's desk. Miss P entered with a large white bag whose aroma made Mac's stomach growl. Having Nate around wasn't all bad.

"Where is everybody?"

"In here." Mac brightened at the sound of her friend's voice. "Bring a chair."

"Yummy." Sam scooted in between Mac and Nate.

God bless her.

"Is there enough for me?" She flashed Nate a big smile.

"Of course." He waved a hand toward the bag. "Help yourself."

Sam dug a burger out and placed it on her plate. "We're thankful you can take so much time away from your practice to help us, Nate."

"I'm between cases right now."

"Us too." Sam took a bite.

Mac wiped her hands and extracted her phone from her pocket. Mr. Fischer's office number showed on her screen. "Excuse me." She rose and left the room. "Mackenzie Love."

"Miss Love? This is Claudia Smith, Mr. Fischer's assistant. I'm afraid I have bad news."

CHAPTER 5

"What's happened?" At Claudia's words, Mac's fingers tightened around her phone.

"He fell down the stairs at work," Smith said. "He's in the hospital with a concussion and a broken hip. I understand he was to meet with you on Sunday."

"Yes."

"He'll have to reschedule when he gets out of the hospital."

"Thanks for letting me know, and please tell Mr. Fischer we're praying for his recovery."

"I will." The phone went dead.

Sam slipped through the door and over to Mac's side. "What is it?"

"Mr. Fischer's in the hospital with a concussion and a broken hip." She stuffed her phone into her jeans pocket. "He took a tumble on the stairs at work. Supposedly."

"Do you think there's more to it?"

"Maybe. Maybe not." Mac lifted her shoulder in a half shrug. "He sets up a face-to-face with us and has an accident, which lands him in the hospital before we can meet."

"What's so unusual? He acted like his problem wasn't a big one, just odd."

"Nothing. I guess." Mac rubbed her arms. "Only a feeling I have."

"Why don't we go visit him in the hospital?"

"Good idea. Let me grab my purse." Mac entered her office to find Miss P and Nate cleaning up the remains of lunch. "Sam and I are going to the hospital. Mr. Fischer's been injured."

"Oh my." Miss P lifted her face, each wrinkle pinched with concern.

"I'll go with you." Nate jammed the paper plates into the trash bag.

Mac flung her hands up in a halting gesture. "No, no. That's okay." She smiled at him to take the sting out of her words. "Miss P needs you here, and I'm sure Mr. Fischer isn't up for meeting anyone new."

"I could wait in the hall." Nate stepped closer.

Mac snatched her purse and retreated out the door before she changed her mind. "We won't be long."

In Sam's SUV, Mac lay her head against the backrest and closed her eyes.

"You're attracted to Nate." Sam signaled and turned left at Fifth Street.

How did she do that? "I don't want to be." Mac threw her hands out, fingers splayed. "I wasn't even sure I wanted to date Jake. Now I want him, but he's unsure about me, and I'm drawn to a man I dated years ago. This romance stuff is for the birds."

"I never thought I'd see you defeated by anything, Mac." Sam steered her SUV into the parking lot of the hospital. "It's okay, my friend. I'd rather have you watching my back in a fight than anyone else."

Warmth rose to Mac's cheeks. "But I'm a wimp when it comes to my love life."

"Exactly." Sam led the way through the hospital doors.

After discovering Mr. Fischer's room number from information, the women headed for the elevator. Mac punched two.

"We're visiting Mr. Fischer. Agreed?" Mac asked. "No questions if he's not able."

"Agreed." Sam held up two fingers. "No questions. Scout's honor."

When the doors opened on the second floor, the women stepped out, and Mac led the way down the hall. *Lord, help me abide by what I agreed to.*

The door was ajar. She knocked and pushed it open. A sense of déjà vu rushed over her. Mr. Fischer lay in the bed. Someone bent over him. Just like a few months ago.

"What are you doing?" Mac charged toward the figure.

"Mac." Sam grabbed her friend. "Stop. She's a nurse."

Heart pounding in her chest, Mac collapsed in a nearby chair and buried her face in her hands.

The nurse brushed her uniform into place with a shaky hand. "What's the problem with your friend?"

"It's a long story," Sam placed a hand on Mac's shoulder. "She saved Mr. Fischer from being killed by a lethal injection in this hospital not too long ago. Seeing you bending over him triggered that memory."

"That came out of nowhere." Mac gulped a steadying breath. "I ..."

"It's okay. We'll work through it together."

Mac glanced at Mr. Fischer. Light snoring put her mind at ease. He hadn't heard a thing. "But I don't think we're going to learn anything here today."

"Doesn't look like it." Sam offered Mac a hand as she pushed out of the chair.

They padded toward the door.

"Mackenzie? Samantha? The weakened, yet still commanding, voice of Mr. Fischer came from behind them.

"I'm sorry if we woke you." Mac led Sam back to the bed.

"You didn't." He pressed the controls to raise his head a bit. "I'm glad you came." He waved them closer with a weak motion of his right hand. "I know this sounds paranoid, but I think someone or something tripped me."

"Tripped you?" Sam placed a hand on his arm. "Why?"

"I can't imagine." Puzzlement tinged every word.

"Do we have your permission to investigate?" Mac asked.

Fischer shook his head. "I don't want you involved yet. Not until we've discussed why I want to hire you." He lay his head back and closed his eyes. "And this isn't the place. Too many interruptions."

"No, sir." Sam patted his arm. "You focus on getting better. Then we'll talk."

"I'm scheduled for an operation tomorrow. They're putting a pin in my hip."

"We'll leave you to get some rest."

"Would you pray with me before you go?"

"Be glad to." Mac and Sam stood on opposite sides of the bed and joined hands with Mr. Fischer.

A STEADY RAIN poured from a slate gray sky as Mac and Sam exited the hospital.

"This weather chills me to the bone." Mac pulled her coat tighter around her body.

"Wait here. I'll come pick you up." Sam flipped the hood on her coat over her head.

"Thanks, but I'll run between the raindrops." Mac splashed after her friend across the parking lot.

Inside Sam's SUV, the smell of damp wool filled the small space while they waited for the heater to kick in and the windows to defog.

"Do you think Fischer fell, or was he tripped?" Sam asked.

"I don't know." Mac combed a hand through her wet hair. "I wish we could examine the stairs. If they used a tripwire or something, there might still be evidence."

"But he doesn't want us anywhere near there." Sam rubbed her arms.

For a few moments, all was quiet except for the hum of the car's heater.

"Mac, I think you need to see someone about what happened with the nurse," Sam said.

"It won't happen again. Besides, I have you to talk to." Mac gave her a half smile.

"But—"

"Not right now, Sam." Mac's stomach knotted. Was she being sucked into the same darkness her sister suffered after their parents died? Shadowy memories from years ago coiled along the edges of her mind.

No. She wouldn't let that happen to her. All she needed was work. She turned away from the concerned look on her friend's face. This recent case would set her straight again.

"I'll be fine, Sam."

CHAPTER 6

Time passed by so fast. Five years ago, Sam agreed to start a private investigation agency with Mac. The first few years had been hard, but they'd managed to pay the bills.

She stepped onto her porch, pulled her sweater tighter, and sipped her coffee. A few tenacious leaves still clinging to the trees swayed in the breeze.

Then came the Eleanor Davis murder case, Mr. Fischer's daughter. She and Mac became acquainted with Fischer while trying to find out who killed Eleanor. In the process of solving the case, Sam and Mac ended in the path of danger more than once. Could this new case put them in harm's way once more? If so, was Sam ready to do it again? Was Mac?

Solving that one put them on the map, so to speak. And brought in a fat check.

But cases like those came with consequences. Some of which they were now experiencing. The incident with the nurse pointed to unresolved issues. Mac seemed to think she could handle them on her own. Sam wasn't so sure.

But how would she know when it was time to insist Mac

get help? Sam raised her face to the sky. "I'll trust in Your guidance."

The door opened behind her.

"You're up early." Alan slid his arms around her waist and drew her against him.

"Enjoying a quiet moment before jumping into the day."

"Is there a lot left to do to get ready for the party? I can help?"

"No." She leaned into his embrace. After four years of marriage, his touch still made her tingle. "Miss P is dusting and vacuuming one last time, and that's about it until the food arrives."

Killer bounced through the door and raced out into the yard.

"I wish I had our dog's energy," she said.

"I think you do pretty good." Alan planted a kiss on her neck. "For a gal your age."

"Hey." She elbowed him in the stomach.

"Oof. Not so hard. Remember, I'm fragile."

"Right. About as fragile as a brick wall." She sat her cup on the railing and pulled him to her. "I love you."

"I love you more," he whispered, his lips pressed on hers.

After a time, Sam sighed. "I could do this all day."

"Me too." Alan leaned in for another kiss.

She put a finger on his lips. "But we have jobs. Remember?"

"Oh, yeah." He released her, but kept his hands on her waist. "What time does the party start?"

"Five o'clock. When's your last client?"

"Four." He stepped back. "I'll pick your mom up and should be able to make it a little after five."

Sam nodded, and her mind switched into work mode. After soaking in the sunlit November morning a moment longer, she called Killer inside and put her cup in the sink. Time to get ready for the rest of her day. It was going to be a good day for their party.

"I'll see you later." Alan kissed her cheek and hurried out the door.

Sam drew in the smell of his aftershave lotion and grinned. God had a marvelous sense of humor. He joined a woman whose idea of exercise was a few hours of shopping with a man who worked as a personal trainer and produced a happily ever after.

Thank You, Jesus.

Sam finished getting ready and gave Killer's head a rub. "Got to go, buddy. Be good."

In the car, her cellphone rang. "Samantha Majors."

"Are you at the office?" Mackenzie asked.

"On my way."

"Good. I don't feel so bad. I'm running late."

"That's fine." Sam stopped at a four-way stop. "There's not much to do until after lunch."

"I may wait to come in. Okay?"

"Sure. Miss P and I can handle the few little things left to do." Something in her partner's voice plucked at a nerve. "Mac, what—?"

"Great. See you later."

Mac was gone. Sam hit redial. It went to voice mail. What was her impetuous friend up to?

MACKENZIE WIPED her sweaty palms on her jeans, switched her phone to vibrate, and stowed it in her handbag. She studied the buff-colored brick buildings of Fischer Industries. It was Saturday, and only a few cars sat in the employee lot. A perfect time to gain entrance and poke around. So why was she so nervous?

After stepping out of her car, she slung her bag over her shoulder. Now or never. She crossed the street with a brisk step and yanked on the front door. She started when it yielded to her touch. At least she wouldn't have to search for an alternative way inside.

Dim lighting cast shadows in the foyer and on the stairs. Creepy. The hair on her neck rose, and she shivered. Mac pulled her phone from her purse and pressed the flashlight button. Mr. Fischer said he tripped on something about four or five steps from the bottom. Mac tiptoed to the stairs and bent to examine the tread.

Nothing seemed unusual. She sat on the stairs and gave a small sigh. If she were trying to trip someone, how would she do it? A wire was the first thing that came to mind, but she couldn't see how. The construction of the stairs ruled it out.

Mac moved her light across the stairs again. A section on the fifth step seemed brighter than the rest. She ran her fingers over it. Smooth. Until she got to the far edge. There, it was very sticky. In fact, she had a hard time pulling her fingers away. She muffled a cry of success.

Using her pocketknife, she scraped some sticky stuff into a baggie and sealed it. She stood and placed it in her purse.

"What are you doing?" A man advanced on her out of the shadows. "Who are you?"

She threw her hand in front of her face to block the beam of his flashlight. How much had he seen? "I'm Mackenzie Love, a private investigator. Mr. Fischer asked me to come over and inspect the stairs where he fell." She held out her card.

He took it and angled the light so he could read the information printed there.

Mac peered at the man. Shadows fell on his face, but she

could make out his general build. He was on the short side of six feet with the hands of a man who did physical labor. Muscled arms and shoulders with a slight pooch in the middle. He didn't look familiar.

He handed her card back and kept the beam of his flashlight on her feet. "Didja find anything?"

"No." Mac waved a hand at him and slipped out the front door. Her heart pounded in her chest, and it was all she could do to keep from running to her car. That was too close. As she prepared to drive away, she hazarded a glance at the building once more.

The man stood on the sidewalk and stared. She noted his brown hair. It was too far to see his eyes.

Mac made a left out of the parking lot onto Pine—away from Main and the front door. A few blocks on Second Street and she'd be at the office. Motion attracted her eyes to the rearview mirror.

A white van pulled in behind her. Like the one her attacker escaped in two days ago. She grabbed her phone.

CHAPTER 7

"Go to the office." Jake snatched his coat off the chair and jogged down the hall. "Call Sam and have her meet you outside. Make sure she's armed. I'll call the closest patrol car." His stomach churned. If anything happened to Mackenzie or Samantha …

Lights and siren blasting, he made it across town in record time. He slowed and killed the noise as he approached. Mac and Sam stood in the yard and talked to his fellow officers while two people dressed in black leaned against a white van with Hazel's Back Porch Catering emblazoned across the side. Jake felt a headache coming on.

He sighed and trudged across the lawn toward his sister and her friend. "False alarm?"

"Sorry." Mac rubbed her neck. "I didn't mean to cause such a fuss."

"Hey." He gestured toward the van. "It could have been the van. It still could." He walked over to the two women in black. "Do you have any credentials?"

They pulled cards from their pockets and handed them to

Jake. He flashed them a smile. "Thanks." He turned to his officers. "Stick around for a while, okay?"

He returned to where Mac and Sam stood huddled together. "I'll be back, but I wanted to let you know the latest. We've got the guy's picture out from St. Louis to Kansas City, and a description of the van." He ran a hand through his hair. "It shouldn't be long until we find him."

For a second, there'd been something fragile in the look Mac had given him, and a part of him ached to gather her into his arms.

AFTER SHE APOLOGIZED PROFUSELY, Mackenzie retreated to her office and left Miss P to direct the caterers with the set-up. She paced like a long-tailed cat in a room full of rocking chairs. Was Sam right? Did she have unresolved trauma from the Eleanor Davis case?

She gazed out the window at the white van. But anyone could have made the same mistake she did. Right? And like Jake said, the bad guys could have disguised their van to look like the caterers. Besides, wouldn't a guy pointing a gun at her count as traumatic?

And there was Mr. Fischer's suspicious fall down the stairs. She retrieved the sticky sample she scraped from the step and went in search of Miss P, her old chemistry teacher and former forensics scientist.

Sam and Miss P admired their large conference table, which served as a buffet table today. The balloons Mac bought, grouped together in the center like a bouquet, lent a colorful festive air.

"You two did a great job." Mac surveyed the beautiful dishes and serving pieces laid out ready for the food.

"Thanks." Sam stepped closer. "It's Miss P. She's amazing."

"Yes, she is." Mac handed her the baggie with the sample. "And I need your help with one of your other talents, Miss P. Sometime soon—after the party—I'd like you to analyze this for me."

"Where did it come from?" Miss P turned the clear plastic bag over in her hands.

"The stairway at Fischer Industries."

"Mackenzie." Sam rounded on her. "Is that where you were today? Even after Mr. Fischer warned you not to?"

Mac stiffened. "I had to check it out, and I found something—something I think may have caused his fall."

"What?"

"There was a sticky substance on the fifth tread from the bottom, but just on the edge. Someone cleaned the rest of the stair."

"You're lucky you didn't get caught, or worse." Sam grabbed her arm.

Warmth crept up Mac's neck into her face, and she dared not look Sam in the eye.

"Mackenzie Love. What are you not telling me?" Sam planted her fists on her hips.

"Nothing." Mac paused. "Really."

"Out with it."

Why did her friend have to be so perceptive? Mac prayed for a distraction, but none came. She glanced at Miss P, who stood to one side, peering at her over her glasses. *No help there.*

"Okay. A guard found me." Mac raised her hands in surrender. "I showed him my card and told him Mr. Fischer asked me to look at the staircase."

"So, he thought you were working for Mr. Fischer?"

"I guess so." She shrugged.

"You lied to him." Sam waggled a finger at her. "What if he checks?"

"He won't."

"What else did he say?"

"He wanted to know if I'd found anything." Mac furrowed her brow. "Not that it was any of his business. I said no and took the opportunity to leave."

"Excuse me." One caterer stood in the doorway to the kitchen. "When would you like us to put the food out?"

Mac could have kissed the woman.

"Let's wait until our guests arrive." Miss P bustled across the room. "Since this is a drop-in affair, I don't expect many to show until later."

"Or should we put out a few things now for early arrivals?" Sam asked as she joined her.

Mac glanced at the clock. "Yikes. I need to freshen up. It's almost time. Sam, where's your mom?"

"Alan is picking her up after he gets off work."

Mac left them to take care of the food and retreated to her office. After she pulled a brush through her long hair, she plunked her make-up bag on the credenza beneath the mirror. A little mascara, a swipe of blush, a touch of lipstick, and she'd call it good.

A loud pop sounded from the other room. She threw herself to the floor with her make-up brush gripped in her hand. For a split second, in her mind, she lay on Fischer Industries' gravel parking lot, waiting for the next shot from an unknown gunman. Her heart hammered in her chest. Another image flashed before her. The back of a car seat. Her sister next to her screaming.

Laughter reached her through the closed door of her office. The images disappeared. She pushed to her feet and brushed the dust from her clothes with shaking hands. If Sam had seen her … but she didn't. Mac turned back to the mirror, more determined than ever to get control of her reactions.

Her door opened, and Sam stuck her head in. "Are you about ready? Guests are arriving."

"I'll be right there." Mac beamed at her and willed her hands to stop shaking.

Sam took her arm as she entered the main room. "Did you hear the balloon explode? Scared me to death."

"I wondered what the loud noise was." Mac kept her tone light.

"I didn't know helium balloons would pop like regular balloons, but they do." Sam released her and greeted people coming through the door.

Mackenzie scanned the space. About a half-dozen friends and neighbors had arrived. She recognized their neighbor, Mrs. White, who worked for the historical society, and the two men who lived in back and helped them clean up last year when their office was vandalized. A few clients from their early days got food. The jukebox they rented played a '60s tune.

From the corner of her eye, she spied Nate as he made his way in her direction. She tensed.

"You look ravishing."

"Thanks." Mac avoided his gaze.

"Do you have any breath mints?" He held a hand in front of his mouth. "I had onions for lunch."

"I've got some in my purse." Mac led the way to her office.

In the dim light of her office, she grabbed her purse and rummaged through it. "I know they're here somewhere."

Nate placed his hands on her shoulders. "Macky, I didn't realize how much I care about you until I saw you again."

The whisper of his breath on her cheek made her heart beat a staccato rhythm in her chest.

He turned her to face him and pressed his lips to hers.

She put her hands on his chest. "Nate, no."

A shadow fell across them as the door to her office opened. "Everything okay in here?" Jake asked.

Nate released her and stepped back.

"I'm getting Nate mints." She turned back to her purse. "Here they are." She pressed them into Nate's hand and gave him a gentle shove toward the door.

Jake stepped aside for him to pass and then approached Mac. "Who was that guy and what happened just now?"

"Nate is Miss P's nephew and new in town. He and I used to date in college. We were only talking."

"Was he bothering you?"

"No." She let her eyes roam over the familiar contours of Jake's face. How would Jake react if he knew Nate had kissed her?

"I hope not." Jake balled his fists. "Or I'll be the next one he'll talk to."

"Gosh, Jake, you say the sweetest things." She batted her eyelashes at him and reached to stroke his cheek. He stepped away, and her stomach knotted.

"Hey you two. None of that." Sam laughed. "Mac, you're needed out here."

As they reentered the party, Sam steered her away from the crowd. "What just happened in there? Nate came out looking like his best friend died."

"He kissed me, and I said no." She watched Jake walk across to Mrs. White. Mac put a hand on her stomach. "It didn't help Jake came in right as Nate and I were parting. Did Nate leave?"

"No. He's still here." Sam nodded toward a group of women by the windows. "He's recovered and is charming the ladies of the Dangerous Reads Book Club."

The news about Nate released a tension she didn't realize

she'd been holding onto, and she took a deep breath. Maybe they would find a way to be friends beyond their past relationship. But what about her and Jake?

"Excuse me. Are you Mackenzie Love?" A tall woman with olive-colored skin and shoulder-length brown hair extended an elegant hand.

"Yes." Mac exchanged a firm shake and smiled at the stranger.

"I'm Claudia Smith, Mr. Fischer's assistant." She folded her hands in front of her. "He asked me to come in his place and to give you—and Mrs. Majors—his regards." She nodded at Samantha.

"Thank you," Sam said.

The woman opened her mouth to say something but seemed to think better of it.

"How long have you worked for Mr. Fischer?"

"About nine months." She continued to stare at Mac.

"Is there something else?" Mac asked.

"I'm sorry to be so rude." Claudia Smith passed a hand across her face. "There's something familiar about you. I can't put my finger on it."

Mac stiffened. "Do I remind you of someone?" Her pulse quickened.

"I can't say. It's more a feeling." Smith shrugged. "I'm sorry. I shouldn't have said anything. Congratulations on your anniversary and I wish you continued success."

"Thank you." A flurry of activity at the front door caught Mac's attention. "There's Alan with your mom."

"Excuse me." Sam hurried away.

Claudia Smith uttered a soft gasp. She'd turned her back on the new arrivals and lifted a hand to her throat. "I believe I'll use your restroom before leaving, if I may."

CHAPTER 8

"Sure?" Unable to keep the question from her voice, Mac pointed in the direction of the bathroom.

After Smith left her, Mac scrutinized the group at the front door again. It was clear Claudia Smith didn't want someone to see her. But who? Alan? Mac couldn't imagine why. Unless … but that was out of the question. And Mrs. Sanders lived in Florida, so it couldn't be her.

Jake? Did Claudia Smith have a criminal history? Or did she know Jake from another time? Could that be the reason he acted so strange? A wave of sadness passed over her. The cluster of people moved her way. Jake flashed her a brief smile with his slightly crooked teeth, and her chest ached.

"Good to see you again, Mrs. Sanders." Mac folded the older woman in her arms and breathed in her rose-scented perfume.

"You too, Mackenzie." She placed a soft hand on Mac's cheek. "It's been too long."

"Yes, ma'am."

"Mom, this is Miss Priscilla Freebody." Sam reached for Miss P. "You remember. I've talked about her to you."

"Of course. You're the wonderful cook Sam raves about—among other things."

Miss P blushed. "I try. These young girls do not eat the way they should."

"I know." Mrs. Sanders took Miss P's arm and walked off.

"I guess we don't have to worry about entertaining Mom," Jake said.

"Nope." Sam slipped her arm through Alan's. "Thank You, Jesus."

"Amen," Alan said. "You're being quiet, Mac. What's up?"

"Something weird happened a minute ago."

"How can you tell? Weird is getting to be normal for you."

"Hah, hah." She scowled at him. "Jake, do you know a woman named Claudia Smith? Olive skin? Shoulder-length brown hair? Tall, elegant?"

Jake's expression narrowed in concentration. After a moment, his gaze returned to her. "No. Why?"

"Do you, Alan?"

"Nope."

"She's Mr. Fischer's new assistant. Sam and I were talking to her when Alan and your mom came in. We turned toward the door, and she started acting strange."

"What do you mean?"

"There's someone here she doesn't want to run into," she said. "I thought it might be one of you because you'd just arrived."

Mac scanned the room. A man standing with his back to her caught her eye. Something about him was familiar. She'd go talk to him in a moment.

"We'll have to revisit this mystery later. Right now, I need to rescue my mom from Nate." Jake threaded his way through a few dancers toward his mother.

"Be kind." Guilt for Jake's attitude toward Nate weighed on Mac. If he hadn't seen them in her office, he wouldn't feel so negative about the guy.

Nate spied Jake headed his way and beat a hasty retreat. Jake steered his mom over to where Mrs. White sat by herself. Mac breathed a sigh of relief. She never realized a party could contain so many emotional landmines. It was exhausting.

The man she'd seen earlier had disappeared, and she was hungry. Hopefully, nothing would keep her from having a bite to eat. She filled her plate to overflowing and searched for a place to sit. A woman rose from a chair by the front window, drink in hand. Mac slid onto the still warm seat and smiled as the far corner of the room erupted in laughter.

As with most gatherings, most people congregated around the food with a few seated in pairs along the sides. They'd cleared a small space for anyone who felt like dancing, and Mac watched as a few couples moved about the floor. Now it seemed like a party. Food, friends, and fellowship.

Ivy, her friend since grade school, crossed the room with a big smile on her face. She held hands with a man in a sports coat. Slim, brown hair, and about six feet tall. His glasses added a scholarly air. A professor at the college?

"Mac, I want you to meet my new guy, Doctor David Quinn." Ivy snuggled against him, and he smiled down at her.

The new doctor in town. Mac stood and put out her hand. "I'm glad to finally meet you, Dr. Quinn. I've heard about you. Hope you're settling in okay."

"With Ivy's help, I'm doing just fine." He grinned at her. "Congratulations, by the way. Ivy talks about you all the time and all your cases. Pretty exciting."

"I'm sure she exaggerates a little." Mac laughed. "Although

we have had a few scrapes here and there. Did she tell you she's worked undercover with me on a couple of those cases?"

"No." He raised an eyebrow at the blushing woman next to him.

"We need to go before you tell him all my secrets." Ivy hugged Mac. "David's got rounds tomorrow morning."

"I'm glad you both came, and that I met you, Dr. Quinn."

"David," he said with a warm smile. "We'll get together when we have more time to talk."

Mac nodded. Once they'd gone, she settled in her chair and took a drink. A slight motion to her left drew her attention. Claudia Smith slipped along the wall behind a group of people. She ran anxious eyes over the crowd before she took three brisk strides to the front door.

What was the woman still doing here? Mac rushed to intercept her, but she was nowhere to be seen. Was she looking for someone? Or hiding from somebody? Mac surveyed their guests once more. The party was winding down, and many had left.

Sam waved her over to the buffet table. "Let's put some of this away. I need to get my mom home."

"You guys should go on," Mac said. "You did most of the prep beforehand. I can handle the clean-up."

"Are you sure?"

"Positive." Mac took Sam by the hand and led her over to where her mom and husband sat in one corner. "Time to take your women home." She flashed a grin at Alan.

"Gladly." He helped his mother-in-law to her feet and gave Mac a weary smile. "Let's go, ladies."

When the caterers cleared the buffet table, the remnant of partygoers said their goodbyes. Mac and Miss P stood by the front door and hugged them on their way.

"I thought my face would get stuck in a smile like that

gross character from one of those movies." Mac flexed her cheeks a few times.

"What would you like us to do with all the balloons, ma'am?" One caterer asked.

Mac raised her eyebrows at Miss P. "Leave them for now?"

"Yes. We can deal with them on Monday," Miss P said. "Is the food in storage containers?"

"Yes, ma'am."

"Be sure to take some home, Mackenzie."

Jake came down the stairs from the second floor. "Are there anymore folding chairs to go upstairs?"

Mac and Miss P glanced around and shook their heads. Mac's pulse quickened. She'd forgotten he was still there.

Miss P turned to him. "Be sure to take leftovers when you leave, Detective."

"Thanks." He threw her a smile. "What else can I do?"

"Trash?" Mac asked.

"No problem."

"The bags are in the kitchen." After he'd left, Miss P smiled. "He's such a nice young man."

"He is." Mac raised a hand to her mouth. So were his kisses. Warmth traveled up her neck. If only she could find out what bothered him.

Nate was nowhere to be seen, and that brought on a very different feeling. Guilt.

"Miss P, I need to talk to you about Nate." Mac touched her friend's arm.

"I understand, my dear." Miss P gave her a sad smile. "I saw him enter and leave your office." She sighed. "I can only guess at what transpired."

"No, nothing happened." Mac took Miss P's hand. "But I think I stepped on his feelings tonight. I didn't mean to hurt him—or you."

"Nonsense." Miss P patted Mac's hand. "What is it your mother said about another person's actions?"

Mac smiled. "She'd say, 'You are not responsible for anyone else's actions, only your own.'"

"Wise words." Miss P released her hand. "Please understand whatever happens between you and Nate has nothing to do with our relationship." She straightened. "Let's get this finished so we can go home and get some rest. I believe this party was a great success."

"Me too." Mac lifted one edge of the tablecloth. "I'll take this home and wash it."

"Where is the area rug for the reception area?"

"In my office. I'll get it in a minute."

"I can get it." One caterer headed for Mac's office door. "I believe we're ready to settle the bill and leave."

"Of course," Miss P said.

A scream sliced the air.

CHAPTER 9

Jake let the back door slam shut and rushed across the room. The woman stood frozen in the office doorway. He pushed her aside. A man exited the room through the window. Pulling his phone from his pocket, Jake ran for the front door. "Suspect seen leaving the house on foot."

"In pursuit."

"Where are you?"

"Headed down Johnson toward Robert."

"Right behind you." Jake strained to see his fellow officer ahead.

A shot rang out in the gathering darkness.

Jake ran toward the uniformed officer lying on the pavement. "Officer down at Johnson near Roberts." He jammed his phone into his pants pocket and knelt beside the unconscious man. A pulse pushed against Jake's fingers. "Williams, can you hear me? Come on, man." Jake gave his shoulder a gentle squeeze.

The man's eyes fluttered open for a second. "I ..."

"Don't try to talk. Help's coming."

Jake stood as emergency vehicles raced in from all directions. More police piled out. "Get the neighbors back." He grabbed one officer. "Take pictures of the crowd." His eyes landed on Mac and Miss P huddled to one side. Mac's eyes held a look filled with compassion. He turned away, his heart pounding in his chest.

Detective Victor Young hurried over. "I got here as fast as I could."

"You take the scene. I'm going with Williams."

The EMTs pushed the gurney to the waiting ambulance, and Jake jogged alongside. "I'll meet you at the hospital." He broke off and headed for his car.

"Jake." Mac reached for him as he passed.

"No time now." He waved her away. "Later." As he sped away, his phone rang.

"Sanders," Chief Baker said. "What's the situation there?"

"Officer Williams is on his way to the hospital."

"How bad?"

"I'm not sure." Jake flew through an intersection. "I left Young in charge, and I'm on my way there now."

"Keep me posted," the Chief said. "Good to have you back, Sanders."

"Yes, sir."

Yeah. Welcome back to chaos, with Mackenzie right in the middle of it. In all fairness, it wasn't her fault—this time. Jake heaved himself out of his car.

He strode through the emergency room doors, and flashes of déjà vu stopped him cold. Once more his heart pounded in his chest as he remembered racing here a little over a month ago, the night of Mac's crash. He willed himself back to the present and the officer he'd come to see.

"I'm Detective Jake Sanders." He displayed his badge to the nurse at the desk. "I'm here to see Officer Williams."

"Room two." She pointed to the double doors to her left. "I'll let you in."

Pain arrowed through Mackenzie's chest as she watched Jake speed away. She longed for things to be different—for him to take her with him. For them to be a team. Was the man who shot Jake's officer the same one who ambushed her in the parking lot?

"Come, dear." Miss P slipped her arm through Mac's. "There's nothing more we can do here. Let's go home."

Mac nodded.

"I'd ask you to come back with me, but Nate is still there," Miss P said. "I'm sure you agree that would not be a good idea."

Mac waved to Miss P, unlocked her car, and drove home on autopilot through the early morning hour before dawn, her mind wrestling with feelings of guilt and sadness. She parked in her driveway and let herself in before realizing her house was dark. No lights shone from the kitchen or living room as usual.

Fear crawled over her skin. She'd seen enough movies to know what not to do. Backing out the door onto her porch, she turned and ran to her car. Once inside, she pressed one on her phone for Jake and, with a trembling hand, started her car.

"Mac? I'm at the hospital." Jake answered after one ring. "What do you want?"

"Sorry. I pressed your number out of habit." She fought to keep her voice steady. "I'll call 911."

"What's wrong?" A note of concern sounded in his voice.

"Someone's in my house."

"Where are you?"

"Sitting in the driveway in my car."

"Move down the block. I'll send an officer."

"I—" She didn't want an officer. She wanted Jake, but she understood. Her chest hurt so bad she found it hard to breathe. "Thanks."

Mac backed down the street to a spot where she could watch her house and wait for the police. She gripped her steering wheel. Tears flooded her eyes, and she swiped them away. She hadn't cried since her parents died.

Mama's voice filled her mind. "You have to have a cutoff point. You have to surrender your relationships to God." Mac let out a deep breath. Mama was right. Time to let go—of Jake and Nate.

A squad car pulled into her driveway, and Mac got out to meet them.

"Miss Love?" They pulled out flashlights and drew their weapons. "Stay here, please."

"Okay." Mac marked the progress of the police through her home by the beams of their lights. Soon they were back on her porch, motioning her to join them.

"Nobody's inside, but whoever was here trashed the place searching for something," one officer said. "We're going to check the outside and see if they cut the lines into the house. Don't move."

Mac pulled her phone from her pocket and pressed the flashlight button. She shone it in the open front door. The officers weren't exaggerating. Her place was a mess. What could anyone hope to find here? She didn't keep any money at home or own anything of great value.

"The phone lines are intact. Where's your breaker box?"

"In the garage."

One officer took off in that direction. Five minutes later, lights came on in the kitchen and living room, displaying the chaos of what had once been her home. A weariness invaded her bones that had nothing to do with the late hour.

"We'll need you to go through everything and make a list of what's missing." The officer scanned the rooms. "There's more down the hall, I'm afraid."

Mac followed the officer to her home office and bedroom. Both rooms lay in shambles. What had taken the thieves a matter of minutes to destroy would take her hours to put back in order. She passed a hand over her brow.

"It's late. I'm going to rest and do it tomorrow."

"Sure." With a last look around, the officers bid her goodnight and left.

Mac pushed everything to one side of her bed and climbed under the covers. She curled into a ball. Scenes from the last few days played through her mind on a continuous loop until, spent, she stepped off the cliff into sleep.

CHAPTER 10

W here was she? Samantha glanced over her shoulder to where Mac usually sat. She twisted her wedding ring and leaned close to Alan. "After the service, let's swing by Mac's and check on her."

Alan nodded. On her left, her mom nudged her leg. Proper young ladies didn't talk in church. Sam sighed to herself. A married woman with an important job, and yet her mother could still make her feel like an unruly teen. Jake grinned at her over their mother's head. Sam threw him an "I'll-get-you-back look."

As they headed out the door, Sam pulled Jake aside. "We're going past Mac's house to check on her. Do you want to come?"

"About Mac." Jake raked a hand through his hair. "I forgot to tell you she had a break-in last night."

"What?" Sam grabbed his arm. "Is she okay?"

"I guess. I didn't respond. I—"

"What do you mean, you didn't respond?" Sam shook him.

"I was at the hospital with Williams," he said in a cold

voice. "You can't expect me to drop everything and deal with your friend's emergencies personally."

"*My* friend?" Sam took a step back. His words hit her like a slap in the face. Maybe Mac was right, and Jake didn't care about her best friend any longer. She tried to lock eyes with him, but he averted his gaze.

Or was something else going on?

"Can you take Mom home for me so Alan and I can go to Mac's?"

"Sure." Jake hesitated. "Let me know how she is. Okay?"

Sam said nothing. If he wanted to know about Mac, he could call her himself. She took Alan's hand and walked off.

They drove in silence for a few minutes. At a stoplight, Alan placed his hand on hers. "What's going on?"

"Jake's either mad at Mac, or he doesn't care about her like he used to." Sam's shoulders sagged. "And that makes me sad."

"I know, babe." Her husband squeezed her hand before returning it to the steering wheel. "But we talked about this. You can't let what happens between those two get you down. They must make their own decisions."

"That's what I keep telling myself." She gave him a wistful smile.

When they were a block away from Mackenzie's house, Alan slowed and let out a low whistle. Piles of boxes lined the curb. The garage door stood open, revealing a long table filled with odds and ends.

"Is Mac moving?"

"No. She had a break-in last night." Sam slammed her car door and waited for Alan to join her. "I think she could use our help."

"Good thing I left my gym bag in the car." He pivoted and jogged back toward the car.

Sam entered the garage and studied the items on the table.

Each one damaged in some way. She stopped at a delicate porcelain vase that had belonged to Mac's mother. A crack ran down the side. Tears pooled in her eyes. Mac had wanted little of her mother's, but for some reason, this vase was special to her.

Sam stepped into the kitchen from the garage and stopped. Jake called it a break-in. This seemed so much worse—more like they needed to bring in the dogs to search for anyone trapped under the debris.

"It's not as bad as it looks."

Sam brought her gaze around to focus on her friend standing in the doorway to the hall. How could she be so calm?

"They didn't break any of the furniture. Only a few small items. I'm collecting them now." Mac wiped a hand across her face.

Upon closer examination, Sam noticed dark shadows under bloodshot eyes. She crossed the kitchen and pulled her friend into a hug. "I'm so thankful you're okay."

"They'd left by the time I got here." Mac disengaged from Sam's embrace. "It was too late to call, and I was beat. I hope you understand."

"Of course." Sam smiled and tears leaked down her face.

"Please don't cry." Mac raised her arms. "You'll get me started, and I've already cried more than I've done in five years." She placed her hands on her hips. "Besides, I've still got a lot of work to do."

"Alan and I are here to help." Sam looked down at her dress. "But I'll need to borrow work clothes."

"What about Alan?"

"He's wearing his gym clothes." Sam wrinkled her nose and laughed.

"Great." Mackenzie chuckled. "We can be smelly together."

MOST SUNDAYS, Jake left church with a feeling of peace and contentment to start his week. But not today. Today he churned with guilt and frustration—about his officer being shot, not being there for Mac, and not spending enough time with his mom. He helped his mother into his police-issued SUV and drove into town.

"Not much of a visit for you so far, is it Mom?" Jake opened the door to Cowan's Restaurant and ushered her inside. They'd beat most of the after-church crowd.

"I'm fine, son." Mrs. Sanders smoothed a hand over her hair and unbuttoned her coat.

"Jake, Mrs. Sanders, good to see you again." Ivy greeted them with a big smile and led them to an empty table. "Will this do?"

"Have you got something away from the windows?" Jake asked. "They can be chilly this time of year.

"Sure."

"This place has changed little since we left." Mrs. Sanders ran her gaze over the room. "Which can be very comforting at times."

"Do you miss living here?" Ivy asked.

"Sometimes. But we've made a lot of good friends in Florida. Thank you, dear." She raised an eyebrow at the waitress. "I met your new beau at the party last night. He's very handsome."

The girl's cheeks flamed. "I never thought I'd be dating a doctor."

"Is it serious?"

"I hope so. I really like him a lot." Ivy handed them menus. "I'll check back in a few minutes for your order."

"I'm glad Ivy's dating a nice young man. I hope it works." Mrs. Sanders studied the menu. "I always liked her."

"Me too." Jake stirred his tea with his straw. He hadn't been paying attention, his mind stuck on what his mom said earlier. "About you living in Florida. If it weren't for your friends down there, I'd have a hard time living as far from you and Dad."

"Jake, your father and I are so proud of you and your sister. You've both found jobs you love and are good at. We'd never want either of you to give those up." His mother smiled at him. "Besides, I feel far less anxious with you on the Washington, Missouri, police force than if you were, say, on the Tampa police force. Or worse."

Jake laughed. "What's worse, in your opinion?"

"Mrs. Allen next door has a daughter who works for Homeland Security." Mrs. Sanders peered at Jake over her glass. "She's on an undercover assignment and can't even call her mother. Can you imagine?"

"You're right. Much worse." Jake bit into his hamburger. He could never do undercover work. Cut off from his family and friends. And Mackenzie. He stopped chewing. Where did that come from?

"And she's such a pretty girl. Tall and slim, with long dark hair," Mrs. Sanders said. "Like Mackenzie. Except—"

"Gloria? Is that you?" An older woman bustled over to their table. "I haven't seen you for years."

Jake stood and pulled a chair out for his mother's friend. As he finished his lunch, he kept a part of his mind on their conversation, while the other puzzled over the last words his mom had said like a Rubik's cube.

CHAPTER 11

Jake stood on the porch with his mom and wrapped her small frame in his arms. "Are you sure you're going to be all right by yourself?" Killer's furious bark sounded inside Samantha's front door.

"Of course." She nodded toward the door and grinned. "I've got a vicious guard dog to protect me."

"Yeah." He laughed. "At least he sounds vicious. He might lick them to death."

"That's all that's necessary." She unlocked the door and bent to pet Killer, who bounced around the foyer with excitement. "Come here, precious."

Jake stepped inside. "Sit."

The dog sat.

"It must be your police officer's voice." Gloria Sanders chuckled. "I suppose I'll have to practice being more commanding."

"Use the tone you used with us as kids." Jake hugged her. "I hate leaving you on your own, but I've got lots of work to catch up on."

"I'm fine." She pushed him away. "I'm tired and need a nap."

"See you later."

She nodded and shut the door.

What she'd said at the restaurant came back to him. He raised his fist to knock, but stopped. He'd speak to her tonight.

In the car, Jake checked in with the precinct to see what was going on.

"Not much. A fender bender at the corner of Pine and Second between a black sedan and a white van. The van took off." The officer paused. "And the forensics team went to the house broken into last night. They didn't find any evidence."

"Do we have an APB out on the van?"

"Yes, sir."

"How about Officer Williams?"

"He's doing good. The bullet missed any vital organs. He's whining to go home, but the hospital wants to keep him another day."

"Thanks. I'm on my way in." Jake pressed End. The house broken into. Mackenzie's house. He should check on her. He wanted to check on her. But would she want to see him? He pulled into the parking lot at the police department.

What should he do? He leaned back and closed his eyes. *Go.* The answer came to him from a place deep within that wouldn't show on any scan of the human body.

He called the precinct again. "Change of plans."

JAKE'S HEART beat in his throat. Was Mac moving? Parked a couple of houses away, he took in the scene before him. Alan and Sam moved in and out of the garage, carrying boxes to the curb.

He jumped out of his car and hurried up the street. "What's going on, sis?"

Sam started.

He drew closer and repeated his question.

"We're helping Mac clear out trash and things she's been meaning to get rid of before the break-in."

Tension eased from his body. "So, she's not moving."

"No, silly." Sam rolled her eyes and started for the house.

Should he follow?

"Are you coming or not?" She called over her shoulder.

Follow.

Sam turned to face him. "It looks a lot better than it did when we got here."

Mac stood in the kitchen sorting through papers in a cardboard box. Some furniture still lay like a pile of blocks in the living room and dining room. A weight settled on his chest. He should have been here last night.

But he needed to be with Williams. How could he be in two places at once?

Jake walked over to Mac. "What can I do?" He prayed she wouldn't tell him to leave.

She studied him for what seemed like minutes. "I'm going through my files to see if anything is missing. If you want to be of use, start putting the furniture in place in there." She inclined her head toward the living/dining rooms. "Get Alan to help you."

"Mac, I ..."

"Don't," she said in a husky voice. "I need to get this done."

A DULL HEADACHE formed between Mackenzie's brows. What was Jake doing here? She didn't have the emotional strength to deal with him now. It was clear he wasn't interested anymore, and all he did was remind her of how much she still cared for him. Her mind yelled *Go away*, but her heart ...

Jake looked at her with—tenderness? And her rebellious heart responded. Mac stared at the paperwork in her hand. It took a moment for her to focus. When she did, she realized she had another misfile. This one research on the employees at Fischer Industries at the time of Eleanor Davis's murder, along with extensive research into Fischer himself.

The folder was labeled Research for a New Roof—which Mac and Sam were in the process of finding out about at the same time. How the papers got into that file was a mystery. She grabbed a clean folder and rectified the mistake.

Her back door opened, and Miss P entered with Nate close behind.

"Sorry we took so long. My aunt needed me at home." Nate did a quick scan of the kitchen, living, and dining rooms. "But we're here now and ready to help." He walked over and gave her shoulder a quick squeeze.

"It would help if you'd wash the dishes and put them away."

Nate rolled up his sleeves. "Dishes it is."

Mac finished checking the few remaining folders in the box and took it back to her office. After placing the files in her cabinet, she returned to the kitchen.

Jake and Alan had most of the furniture in place. Clean dishes sat in her cabinets once more, and her home was almost normal again. She rolled her head and shoulders as the tension eased from her body. What would she do without friends?

"Hey, guys. Are you hungry? I'm starved," she said.

"I'm not surprised." Samantha laughed. "You're always hungry."

"We missed lunch." Mackenzie raised a hand in her defense.

"We did," Alan said. "So, what would you like?"

"Burgers and fries, of course. I've got soft drinks and water in the fridge."

"I'll go." Jake headed out the door.

Sam polished the dining room table and put the chairs in place. "This will be like old times."

Mac's heart lurched in her chest as she remembered past dinners with the group. She missed the easy friendship they all had. Maybe tonight would help them get back to that place again.

"HERE YOU GO." Jake entered the kitchen with bags of burgers and fries.

The aroma had her licking her lips.

"I closed your garage door," Jake said.

He touched her hand as he reached for a plate, and a spark radiated up her arm. She glanced at him. Did he feel it too?

"Thanks for closing the garage," she said. "It's getting dark."

At last, they were all seated. The food tasted so good. Probably because she hadn't eaten all day, but as she looked around the table, she knew it had more to do with who she was eating with than what she was eating. These were her friends. Old and new.

"How's Officer Williams doing?" Sam asked.

"He's okay. No major damage and he's already giving the hospital grief about going home."

No one talked for a while as everyone concentrated on their food.

Mac swallowed a bite. "Do you think the guy in my office was my attacker?"

"I'm not sure." Jake shot her a grim look.

"Was he there to kidnap me?" A lump formed in her throat. "Or worse?"

"Who knows, Mac? From the looks of it, he was about to search your office. He may be the same guy who did this to your house."

"But why?" She scanned the faces of her friends, hoping for an answer. "If he thinks I'm someone else, then who? Have any of you seen anyone who looks like me? That he could mistake me for?"

Heads shook around the table.

"It makes no sense." She pushed away from the table. "How can I protect myself against something when I have no clue what it is? How can I stop it? What am I supposed to do? Take out a billboard that says, 'You've got the wrong girl.'?"

"Possibly your break-in was because they suspect you're not the woman they're after," Miss P said. "They may have been searching for evidence they have the right person—or the wrong person."

"If that's the case, I pray they found it and stop coming after me." Mac scooted back to the table and pulled her plate in front of her. "I'm pretty sure the whole furniture thing was to hide what they were really after."

"Me too," Jake said. "When Alan and I put the living room and dining room back to rights, all we found were minor scratches on a couple of pieces."

Mac nodded. "I think they were after something in my home office."

"You went through all your files. Did you find anything missing?"

"No," she said. "But there were papers misfiled. One of

those might have been what they were interested in. I put them aside to study later."

Jake rose and gathered his trash. "I need to go. Early morning tomorrow and still piles of paperwork on my desk." As he passed Mac, he leaned close. "Walk with me to my car."

Her throat closed, and she laid her half-eaten sandwich on her plate. At least Jake had the courtesy to end their budding relationship in person and in private. She stood and steeled herself for what he was about to say.

Nate moved close so no one else could hear. "Don't make any hasty decisions."

She stared at him. What did he mean?

CHAPTER 12

Mac sensed Jake waiting for her in the shadows, and her heart sped up. The scent of his aftershave threatened to crack her defenses. He raised a hand as if to touch her face. She shied away.

"I want to apologize. For not being here when you called me." He stuffed his hands into his pockets. "And for behaving the way I have since I've been back."

"No problem." She wrapped her arms against her body. "You needed to be with your officer, and we hadn't made any promises to each other."

He narrowed his gaze. "I thought ... well, I thought it was understood we would pick up where we left off when I got back."

She raised a shoulder. It was the closest she could come to a casual shrug, and it cost her. She wasn't sure how much longer she could do this.

"Let me explain." He touched her. "I watched my mom grieve for my dad—"

Grieve? "Your father's dead?" She reached for him. Why

hadn't Sam told her? The loss of a loved one left a special scar, and Mac's heart ached for her friends.

"No, but he might as well be." Jake took her hand. "After over fifty years of love, he doesn't know who Mom is." His eyes glistened in the soft light of the moon. "It tore me up. I didn't realize how much until I got back."

He pulled her closer. "I thought I could stop the hurt by simplifying my life. Stop dating, concentrate on work, and just be friends, but I can't deny how I feel about you." He caught loose hairs blowing in her face and tucked them behind her ear. "But I need time, Mac. Time to heal. Do you understand?"

The wall she'd constructed around her heart shattered.

"Yes." She swallowed past the lump in her throat.

He bent to kiss her, but she pushed him away.

"Don't. I can't ..." She tapped a finger against his chest. "Figure out what you want first. Friendship or something more."

"I understand." He gave her a sad smile and left.

Mac brought a hand to the cheek Jake's fingers touched. He still cared about her. A smile touched her lips. Now if she could follow her own advice and figure out what she wanted.

She stepped inside. "Did you save my hamburger?" Sam and Miss P stood at the kitchen sink. Where was Nate?

Mac heard something down the hall to her left and followed the sound to her office. Nate stood with his back to the window.

"Were you spying on me?" A sudden flash of anger shot through her. She crossed the room in two strides and poked a finger in Nate's chest. "You have no business being in here without my permission."

"Sorry." He held a hand up in surrender. "I ..." He pulled her into his arms and took her lips in a soft kiss.

She stiffened and pushed away from him. "That's not fair."

"Do you love him?"

"And that's none of your business."

"It is if I'm in love with you."

"Are you?"

"Yes."

Mac backed away. "I don't believe you." She shoved him out the door. "Don't you ever come in my office here or at our business again without being invited. Do you understand?"

"Yes." He gave a slow nod.

She placed one hand on her forehead and one on her hip. "Leave. Now."

"But I've got something important to tell you."

"I don't care if you know when the sun's going to explode." She threw up her hands. "Right now, I want you out of my sight." She was tired of dealing with men.

"Okay. You're tired. We'll talk tomorrow." Nate turned to his aunt. "Aunt P?"

"We'll give your aunt a ride later." Mac herded him to the door. "We've got work to do."

"Mac, I'm sorry." His gray eyes filled with regret. "I meant what I said, but I should have used a different approach. And I do have something important to talk to you about."

She'd overreacted. She was tired.

"Go home. We'll talk tomorrow," she said, her tone soft but firm.

Nate was the second man in her life she'd sent away tonight. She locked the door and turned.

"What mischief was my nephew up to now?"

"It's nothing." Mac joined them in the kitchen. "I overreacted."

"My dear, do not be sorry." A puzzled look passed over Miss P's face. "My sister passed away seven years ago. It's been a long time since I've seen Nathanial, but I'm rather surprised at his behavior."

"Me too," Mac said.

"You said we had work?"

"Yes. I need your help to go through some files." Mac led the women down the hall to her office. "Something tells me whatever the guy was looking for is in here." She ran a hand over the box with the misfiled folders. "But I'm worn out. I'd like fresh eyes on these files."

She handed each of the women two folders. "Please go home, read through these, and see if anything jumps out at you. Put them in another bag. There may be someone watching my house."

Sam uttered a sharp cry. "You can't stay here by yourself. Come home with Alan and me."

"I'll be fine. Jake left an officer outside for the night." She crossed her fingers behind her back. "We'll meet here in the morning. I don't know when the police will let us into our offices again."

After her friends had left, Mac checked all the door and window locks before heading for her bedroom. Every fiber of her being cried out for sleep, but she still had to get her bedroom straightened up—or shove it aside and crawl into bed like she did last night.

Another thing left until tomorrow. She flipped the light on in her bedroom and gasped. Before her stood a neatly made bed. No clothes covered the floor, and one of her wonderful friends replaced all the drawers in her dresser and chest of drawers.

Mac opened the door to her closet. Her blouses hung in an orderly row, sorted by color alongside her pants. Had to be Miss P. She'd seen Sam's closet skills.

Her eyes were drawn to the chair sitting in the corner with

the small bookcase and lamp next to it. There was one more thing she needed to do before going to bed. She sat down and pulled a worn Bible from among the books.

THE VISION of Mac's lips stayed with Jake all the way home. He knew what it felt like to kiss her, and that was the problem. Was it love he felt for her or strictly physical attraction? Like Mac said, he had a lot to figure out.

He slid through his front door. Now that he knew his cat, Duke, was really a Duchess, he didn't like the idea of her going outside the house. Before, he figured "he" could take care of "himself," but now Jake felt protective. Ouch. That pinched him on his sexist nerve.

Was that part of the problem with Mac? Did he want to put her in a bubble so he could protect her?

"Mwarw." A sleek gray cat padded across the floor and rubbed against his leg.

"Do you miss going outside?" Jake held the cat and gazed into her bright green eyes.

She squirmed.

"I bet you do." He held her to his chest and stroked her fur. "After dinner, I'll open your door again."

She purred and nuzzled her head against his arm.

Jake watched her eat with dainty bites and wondered how he could have missed the fact this elegant creature was female. When she finished, he walked to the back door, squatted, and unlatched the cat door.

She strode over, sniffed, and brushed against his leg. Then she was gone into the night.

Jake kneaded his chest where it ached. "Come home safe."

After a shower and a bite of dinner, Jake reclined in his

favorite chair and tuned his television to the news. But his concentration kept wandering back to what his mom said at lunch about her neighbor's daughter.

Tall, slim, long dark hair like Mac. Working undercover for Homeland Security. Mac's mysterious look alike? He rubbed his eyes. He must be tired to even think that. Besides, he hadn't seen anyone who resembled Mac in Washington, Missouri. Much less a Homeland Security agent.

CHAPTER 13

Sam's tired face relaxed into a smile as she watched her sweet dog through her kitchen window. Killer assumed the play position in front of his ball, grabbed it, and tossed it into the air.

Alan came behind her.

"Do you think dogs have imaginary friends?" she asked.

He laughed. "It sure looks that way."

She turned in his arms. "Are you gone all day?"

"Most of it. I thought I'd come home to have lunch with your mom."

"Thanks. I'll be gone this morning, too." She moved away. "I'm not sure when I'll get back. But I'm taking tomorrow off. I don't care what happens."

"You don't have to take any time off on my account." Gloria Sanders pulled out a chair at the kitchen table. "I'm fine. As for today, my friend, Winnie, is taking me shopping and out to lunch. We ran into each other after church yesterday."

"Great, Mom." Sam raised her eyebrows at Alan. "I guess I'll get ready."

In their bedroom, Alan grabbed her and pulled her close.

"You're impeding progress, mister." She giggled.

"Hmm." He nuzzled her neck. "Are you feeling better about your mom's visit?"

"I am. She seems to be fine. Relaxed."

"Everybody needs a break once in a while."

"Yeah." Sam kissed her husband.

"Now who's holding up progress?" He gave her a gentle nudge toward the bathroom.

What would she have done without this man? The time she spent in Florida with her mother and father left her emotionally drained. She brushed on mascara and examined her reflection in the mirror.

The sallowness to her skin was gone, and the dark circles under her eyes had almost disappeared. If she hadn't had Alan to come home to, Lord knows where she'd be. She leaned in to apply lipstick and paused.

Could that be part of Jake's problem? He had no one waiting at home for him except his cat. His relationship with Mac hadn't developed enough for him to turn to her for support.

Sam's heart ached for her brother. Why hadn't she thought of that before? She finished her routine and made a mental note to talk to him as soon as possible.

Now she needed to get to Mac's and figure out who was after what from her best friend. Sam kissed her husband, her mom, and her dog in that order, and steered her car for Mac's house once more.

Miss P's large sedan sat on the street when Sam arrived—which was no surprise. The woman made a habit of arriving early. When Sam stepped inside, her heart sent a smile to her lips. Mac's home was back together.

She did a little dance around the living room into the dining room, and deposited her bag on the table.

Miss P chuckled.

"Enough Ginger." Mac growled. "We've got work to do."

Sam sat with a contented sigh. The gang was back to normal.

"What did you two find—if anything—in the files you took home?"

Sam drew her folders out of her bag along with her computer. "The only item of interest was the stuff we collected on Fischer Industries last year."

"Why would you classify the Fischer file as interesting?" Miss P asked.

"I guess because Mr. Fischer has something he wants us to work on now." Sam raised her eyes to Mac. "Have you heard anything from him?"

"Yes. He called this morning." Mac scratched her nose. "He's coming here at two this afternoon."

Sam's pulse sped up. "We should review this file before he gets here."

Mac nodded. "But first, was there anything in the two folders you looked at, Miss P?"

"Not really. One held copies of your college newspaper."

"I kept a subscription for several years after I graduated." Mac rolled her eyes. "I wanted to keep up with the people I knew and see what they were doing. I can't imagine those moldy old newspapers could be of any importance to anyone but me. I'm not even sure why I kept them."

Something stirred in Sam. "Can I read them?"

"Be my guest." Mac snorted. "If you're having trouble falling asleep, these could be the antidote. After you're done, you can throw them out."

"But for now, we read the file on Fischer Industries." Miss P picked up the folder and portioned the pages out among the three of them.

MAC OPENED the door and ushered Mr. Peter Fischer into her home. The man who once carried himself with military bearing now leaned heavily on his cane. His gray hair seemed duller, as did his blue eyes.

"Thank you for seeing me on such short notice."

However, his commanding voice remained the same. Mac smiled to herself.

"Please, sit down." She motioned to her couch and chairs. "Would you like something to drink? Water? Tea? A soft drink?"

"Water please." He made his way over to where Miss P and Sam were standing. "I don't believe we've met." He extended his hand to Miss P.

"I'm Priscilla Freebody, Mr. Fischer. I work with Mackenzie and Samantha."

"Ah yes. Of course." After a brief handshake, he smiled at her. "The famous chemistry teacher."

A blush bloomed on Miss P's neck and face. "If you say so, sir."

"Hello, Mrs. Majors." He took her hand. "Good to see you again."

Mac wouldn't have been surprised to see Sam drop into a curtsy, but she restrained herself. "Here's your water. Shall we sit?"

Sam helped Mr. Fischer ease into a chair and then joined Mac on the couch. Miss P took the other chair.

"It seems like a long time since I first called you about my problem." Mr. Fischer folded his hands in his lap. "I'm not sure where to begin."

"Anywhere will be fine." Mac nodded at Sam, who picked up a pad and pencil from the cushion next to her.

"Things have been happening at the office—odd things." A puzzled look slid across his face.

"What sort of things?" Mac asked.

"Items being moved in my office or a desk drawer ajar when I know I closed it." He took a sip of water. "Nothing ever appears to be missing, but someone has definitely been in there."

"There is a simple fix. Install cameras."

"I have cameras." He barked a laugh. "Whoever it is, can disable them when necessary."

"Fingerprints?"

"Our security men cannot find any."

"Is it limited to your office?"

"No. My son's office—he's my Chief Operating Officer—and one or two of the labs as well. Things missing only to be found in odd places."

"Is there something new you're involved in right now?"

Fischer's gaze drifted away from them. "No, not really."

He lied to them. Why?

"Do you think the attempt on your life is related to all these other incidents?" Mac studied his face.

"My fall was an accident." He waved a hand in the air. "I was on a lot of painkillers. I apologize for sounding dramatic."

"No apology necessary." Alarms sounded in Mac's head. "We'll come by later this week and check out your office and the other sites for you." She stood.

"Thank you. You two have special talent—an intuition, a different way of looking at things."

Sam helped Mr. Fischer get to his feet.

He gave Miss P a small smile. "It was nice to meet you."

Mac and Sam stood at the window and watched Fischer's car drive away.

"What do you think?" Sam asked.

"I think we haven't heard the whole truth, and that bothers me." Mac turned to Miss P. "Have you analyzed the stuff I gave you?"

"Yes. The substance you collected from the stair at Fischer Industries is a much stronger version of the glue used on flypaper." Miss P cocked an eyebrow. "I wouldn't be surprised if it pulled his shoe off his foot when he fell."

"Not an accident."

"I'm afraid not. Although whether the miscreant meant to kill Mr. Fischer or merely scare him, I can't say."

"So, another case where there's the possibility of danger." Sam collapsed onto the sofa. "But if we don't help him, they may hurt Mr. Fischer."

"He could still be in danger, even if we help with whatever this is." Mac chewed on her bottom lip. "And we could end up in trouble, too."

"Or not." Sam straightened. "We are good at what we do."

"Ever the optimist." Mac plopped next to her. "Okay. We go to Fischer Industries and investigate Mr. Fischer's problem. But the minute people start getting hurt, we're done. Agreed?"

"Agreed."

Mac's phone chimed, and Jake's name flashed on her screen.

"I'm coming over. We need to talk," he said.

"Hello to you too," Mac said, but the line was dead.

"I'm leaving before my brother gets here." Sam slipped on her jacket and snagged her bag.

"I get it. I'll talk to you in the morning." Mac put the notebook in a drawer and straightened the sofa cushions.

"Miss P, you should go home too before Nate shows up, checking to see if you're okay."

"I'm meeting him for dinner in a half hour. I'll help clean until it's time to leave."

Sam hugged the two women and left. Mac closed the door and turned on the porch light.

"Miss P, when was the last time you saw Nate before now?" Mac picked up a glass and headed for the kitchen.

"I believe it must have been his college graduation—seven years ago."

"He was a year ahead of me." She rubbed a slight ache in the center of her chest as she remembered that time in her life. She and Nate said their goodbyes before graduation, and she left for home the day before. "He must have gone to law school right after."

"I wouldn't know." Miss P carried two more glasses into the kitchen. "My sister, his mother, passed away a few months later, and I'm ashamed to say I lost track of him." Regret clouded her features. "I was thankful he renewed our relationship. Now I must go. I'll see you tomorrow."

Mac waved once more at Miss P and closed the door. She regarded her silent house and pressed a hand to her stomach. Would she ever feel safe here again? It would take time—and a state-of-the-art alarm system.

The doorbell rang. She jerked, muscles tense and heart pounding. A hard knock.

Jake. She'd forgotten he was coming. "Sorry. I was busy." She opened the door.

A man sprayed something in her face while another man grabbed her around the waist.

CHAPTER 14

Jake's jaw tightened when he saw a dark green van back out of Mac's driveway. He stared as it passed him, headed for town. The shadows of late afternoon and the van's tinted windows prevented him from seeing the driver, but he felt a stone in the pit of his stomach. Acting on instinct, he made a U-turn and took off after it. He strained to make out a license number. None.

"Dispatch, this is Detective Sanders. I'm in pursuit of a suspect vehicle on Seventh Street—now turning south on High Street. Dark green late model Honda van. No plates." Jake dropped back a little more. "Do a safety check on Mackenzie Love and get me some back-up. I'm about to stop the van for an improper license."

Jake needed to stop them in the next couple of blocks. If the van made it to Highway 100, it could mean a high-speed pursuit, putting a lot of people in danger. He pressed the accelerator.

Before he could pick up speed, a truck darted across the intersection in front of him. The frightened teenage driver threw up his hands as Jake's police vehicle careened into the bed of his pickup and sent him spinning.

"Detective Sanders? Are you there?"

Jake released his belt and retrieved his phone from the floor. "Yeah. I'm here."

"What happened?"

"Some idi ... young man decided to see if he could beat me across the intersection." Jake let out a disgruntled sigh. "And we both lost."

"Do you need assistance?"

"Not me, but my vehicle is going to need a wrecker." Jake ran a hand down his face. "Did anyone check on Miss Love?"

"Yes, sir. Her door was wide open, but she wasn't home."

Jake's head pounded. "Put out an APB on the van. Now." A hard lump of fear formed in his stomach as the realization of what was at stake dawned on him. He could lose Mac forever over a case of mistaken identity.

Mac kept her eyes closed and listened as the van bounced along the road. She had no idea how long she'd been out and, unlike heroines in books and movies, she wasn't able to tell where she was by road sounds.

When she got out of this, she and Sam should drive each other around blind folded and practice. She felt a giggle rise in her throat and forced it down. Who was she kidding? This was it. The real deal. When they found out she wasn't who they thought she was, they'd kill her.

Sam would say, "Not so fast, girlfriend. We're licensed private investigators. We have skills." But all Mac's skills required she have her hands and legs free—which they were not. And when they were? She'd see.

The van made a sharp left, and a garage door screeched. *Honey, we're home.*

"You can stop pretending to be asleep." The man with the scar yanked her to a sitting position.

As he did so, the cross dangling from her neck caught on something, and the delicate necklace fell off in the van. He undid the ropes around her ankles. "We're at our first stop. Get out."

Mac stumbled as she stepped out of the van and fell against her other captor. "I don't feel good."

"Get inside." He squeezed her arm.

"Ow. You're hurting me." She tried to pull away from him, but he glared at her, one eye cloudy.

Cloudy Eye steered her down a short hall and into a small bedroom, where he pushed her onto the bed. "Toilet in there." He motioned through another door. "Food in an hour."

When Mac had fallen against the man by the van, she'd done a quick check of the pockets she could reach. Nothing. Not even a paperclip. Although why someone like him would carry a paperclip …

She rose and inspected the bathroom first for any sharp edge she could use to cut the tie around her hands. No joy. Then the bedroom. She was about to give up when something pricked her finger as she ran it along the baseboard behind the bed.

Working it carefully out of the space between the wall and the baseboard, Mac discovered a piece of broken glass. She wrapped it in the hem of her blouse and sawed at her constraints.

The door burst open. She dropped the piece of glass onto the bed and placed her folded hands on top.

"Your meal. You should be able to manage with your hands

tied." The man eyed her. "I'll be back in fifteen minutes to pick up the tray."

Keeping her head bent, Mac waited for him to leave. When he had gone, she placed the fragment of glass under the mattress. She ate as much of the food as she could and sat on the floor propped against the wall until time for bed. She noticed something else that could come in handy. One of the wooden slats under the bed was loose.

"It is time to sleep." The men came in with a needle.

"You don't have to do this." Mac cringed in the corner. "I promise I'll sleep. I won't give you any trouble."

"Orders."

"From whom?"

"Your father."

"My father's dead. I'm not who you think I am." Mac kicked and squirmed as they pinned her to the bed.

"Stop or we will tie your legs, too."

"Silly girl, don't you realize your father is trying to protect you?"

"But I keep telling you. My father is dead." Mac peered at the one with the scar. "Ouch." She swiveled her head to Cloudy Eye. "You have the wrong ..."

CHAPTER 15

Mac woke, the sheet damp with drool beneath her cheek. She swung her legs over the edge of the bed and sat up. A tray with congealed oatmeal, a banana, and a bottled water sat on a small table, the only other piece of furniture in the room besides the bed.

The room appeared to have no windows. She had no way of knowing what time it was. Most likely morning judging by the food, but early or late, she couldn't tell. Her wrists chafed under the plastic cuffs, and she remembered the glass fragment. Had they found it?

Still there. She tucked it into her waistband and went into the bathroom. The door had no lock, but it closed tight, and she doubted they'd disturb her. She hoped. After removing the glass shard from her pants, she sat on the toilet, wrapped her shirt around it, and set to work on the cuffs once more.

The door opened to her room. She froze.

"You haven't touched your breakfast. Are you okay?"

"I just woke up. Whatever you gave me was strong."

She flushed the toilet. "I need to wash up."

"I will check on you in a few minutes."

Mac waited for the sound of the door and sawed at her restraints again. *Dear God, help me.* The glass cut her fingers through her blouse, but she grit her teeth against the pain. She had to get free.

When her hands sprung free, the glass slipped in her grasp, and she caught it before it hit the floor. Blood poured from her injured fingers. She tore a strip from the bottom of her blouse and wrapped them. She was ready.

She positioned herself behind the door, the glass shard replaced with a wooden slat from under the bed. The man pushed the door open and stepped over to the closed bathroom door.

"Are you still in—"

Mac slammed the piece of wood against the base of the man's skull as hard as she could. He raised his hand to the spot where she hit him as if a fly had bitten him and turned to face her. What was this guy's head made of? Steel? She brought her leg up to drive a kick into his stomach when his eyes rolled back in his head, and he toppled over like a redwood.

Without waiting for an invitation, Mac grabbed his gun and ran out into the hall. Where was Scar Face? She hurried along the hallway with her back to the wall. An open staircase led down to the first floor. She stooped and surveyed as much of the space below as she could see. Still no sign of the second kidnapper.

She was playing a dangerous game. The man upstairs would wake soon. She needed to get out of there. But she didn't want to run into the other guy. She took her chances and scurried down the stairs.

Something told her to go out the back. She ran through the house on the balls of her feet. There it was. She was free. *Thank you, Jesus.*

Except she had no idea where she was. She paused on the back porch to take her bearings.

Jake grabbed his phone, his heart racing. "Give me some good news."

"A green Honda van, no plates, was spotted on Highway 100 headed east at about the time you had your accident," Detective Young said. "Unfortunately, they lost it in traffic."

Jake raked a hand through his hair. He wanted to jump in his car and drive north on Highway 100, but he curbed the impulse. Police in two states were acting as his eyes. It didn't get any better than that.

And yet.

"I want to speak to my brother." Samantha's irate voice could be heard throughout the precinct.

A weight descended on Jake's chest. He'd prayed they'd find Mac before he had to tell his sister what happened. "Send her in," he said into the intercom.

"Where is Mac? What did you do to her?" Sam stormed into his office and leaned on his desk, facing him.

Do to her? A flash of anger tore through him. For the last twelve hours, all he'd done was rip himself apart for not getting to her house sooner.

He jumped to his feet and stood nose-to-nose with his sister. "I. Didn't. Do. Anything. To. Her."

They remained that way for a moment, staring into each other's eyes. Then Sam collapsed in the chair behind her and dissolved into tears. Regret became a physical pain inside Jake's heart, and he squatted by her side.

"I'm sorry."

"Me too." Sam threw her arms around his neck. "I know

you didn't do anything. It's just that when I got to Mac's house and all those police were there and they wouldn't tell me anything, I got scared."

"I know," Jake said. "Sis, I've got to stand."

"Oh. Sure." Sam pulled her arms back and sniffed.

"You have a right to be worried." He rose and handed her a box of tissues. "Somebody kidnapped Mac."

"When? By whom?"

Anguish emphasized every wrinkle on his sister's face, making her look far older than her years, and it broke his heart.

"It happened last night. I was too late to stop it, but I saw the vehicle pull out of her driveway." He rubbed the back of his neck. "I followed it until some ... teenager got in my way, and we collided."

With every word, he watched her sink further into her chair.

"Do you have any idea where she is now?"

"None. The van headed east on Highway 100." He willed himself to be positive, for Sam's sake. "But every police officer in two states has a description. It won't be long before we hear something."

She pushed to her feet. "I trust in you, Jake, and I'll be praying."

He hugged her and escorted her to the front desk. Once she was out of earshot, he turned to the officer on the phones. "Any news?"

She shook her head.

THE HOUSE SEEMED to be in the middle of a forest. Mac had to decide. Right or left? Again, she prayed for guidance. Right.

The door opened behind her. She spun on her heels and pulled the gun from her back. But she was too late.

"Do you think I have only one pistol?" Cloudy Eye knocked the gun from her hand and grabbed her by the arm. "I've had enough of your mischief. Why your father wants you back is a mystery to me. You are nothing but trouble. Get inside."

He kicked a solid oak chair away from the kitchen table and handcuffed Mac to the arm. "I will make you something to eat —even though I wouldn't care if you starved to death."

Tires sounded on rocks outside. The front door opened and closed. "Michael, I have new orders from the boss." Scar Face stopped short when he saw her in the kitchen. "What is she doing down here?"

"She got her hands free and attacked me." He threw a scowl at Mac. "But, I have a hard head and caught her before she got away."

"Good." The man with the scar took out his phone and pointed it at Mac. "Look at me."

She glanced at him, and he snapped a picture.

"Now we will know if you are speaking the truth."

"Of course I've been telling you the truth." A fragile bubble of hope rose in her soul.

"Here." Cloudy Eye slammed a plate down. "I made you a sandwich."

Mac picked it up and took a bite. She swallowed. "Just tell me why you had to trash my house. What were you looking for?"

"We did not touch your house," Cloudy Eye said. "Our orders were to snatch you and bring you here."

"Then who ...?" She chewed slowly.

A text came through on Scar Face's phone. The look on his face told her all she needed to know. Her throat closed, making it hard to swallow.

"It seems you have been telling the truth." His phone rang, and he stepped into the other room. "Yes." Pause. "Do not put this on us. If you'd told us before, we would never have made the mistake." Another pause. "So, what do we do with the girl?" He glanced back at Mac. "I understand."

Mac's pulse ratcheted upward as adrenaline flowed through her system. She wouldn't go down without a fight.

CHAPTER 16

Finally, news he could act on. Jake grabbed his keys and headed for his vehicle. Someone spotted a van matching his description at a gas station in Dittmer, Missouri. The attendant said it turned down Highway Y. The local police had cars searching the streets and a helicopter scanning the area.

"Young, let's go." Jake signaled to his partner. "They've found where Mac is."

"Great." Detective Young snatched his vest off the hook and caught up with Jake on the stairs. "Where are they?"

"Somewhere near Dittmer. You drive. I want to monitor the radio."

"Dittmer?" Vic slammed the SUV into drive and took off. "That's not very far away. Wonder why they stopped there."

"Who cares as long as we find Mac." Safe and untouched, Jake added to himself. His fingers hovered over a text message to Sam. No, better wait until he knew more.

"I know, Miss P, but there's nothing we can do but pray." Sam hugged her waist a little tighter. "I'm staying home today. Why don't you do the same?" The view from her kitchen window blurred as her eyes filled with tears once again. "I'll let you know any news the moment I hear. And please try not to tell Nate. I know it may be unavoidable, but the last thing Jake needs is Mac's ex barreling into his office like I did."

She hung up and dropped onto a kitchen chair. Killer laid his head on her lap and gazed at her as if he understood exactly how she felt. Sam missed her mother, but Gloria was on a two-day women's retreat with the ladies from church. She yearned to call Alan, but he had back-to-back clients today and she didn't want to disturb him.

"Just you and me, Killer." She rubbed her dog's head. "A walk will help pass the time until Jake finds Mac." It helped to think positive.

Sam lifted the leash and harness from its hook, and Killer stood obediently by her side. Once through the gate, she again let him take the lead. The day suited her mood. There was a bite to the wind, and the trees seemed barer than a few days ago. No bird song cheered her on her way.

Killer led her at a rapid pace toward the spot where they stopped last time. It was clear he wanted to go farther.

"Okay, Killer, we'll do some exploring. Only because it will take my mind off Mac."

The powerful dog lunged forward, yanked the leash from her hand, and took off.

"Killer. Get back here." She used her most commanding voice. To no avail.

She continued to call to him as she strode down the trail. He ran back to her, barking and tail wagging, and turned to run away again. He looked at her over his shoulder. As if he meant for her to follow him. So she did.

As Sam turned a bend in the trail, she spied a tent among the trees to her left. Killer plunged through the brush toward the campsite. She searched for an easier way in and found a break a few feet away.

"Hello. Anyone at home?" She laughed to herself. If anyone had been there, surely they would be out by now with her big lunk of a dog nosing around. She stepped into the clearing by the campfire. It seemed like a regular campsite to her.

Killer crouched at the opening to the tent and whined.

Sam walked over and put her hand on the zipper. "Something tells me I shouldn't be doing this." A shiver ran down her spine. She glanced at her dog. "Stay." She pushed the flashlight button on her phone and slowly opened the flaps.

The smell of unwashed clothes and stale food hit Sam first. Piles of clothing, a knapsack, and shoes were scattered along one side. When she moved her light to the narrow cot in the back, she started. The still form of a woman lay dressed for the outdoors. Was she sleeping? Or ... Sam didn't want to think about the alternative.

"Miss," Sam called in a low voice. "I'm sorry to bother you, but my dog ..."

Nothing.

Sam stepped closer. The woman could be hurt or sick. She reached for the woman's wrist. Was she feeling a faint pulse, or her own blood pounding through her body? Because right now, Sam felt like she could faint herself.

What should she do? Sam bent close to the woman on the cot and smoothed her tangled dark hair away from her face. "Aaahhh!" Sam fell backwards onto the ground, where she pushed herself away from the vision before her.

Killer crashed through the flaps of the tent, teeth bared and hair bristling along his back.

"It's okay, boy." Sam grabbed him around the neck—as

much for her own comfort as to comfort him. Mackenzie Love lay on the cot before her—only somehow Sam knew it wasn't Mac. She prayed it wasn't Mac. Especially if this woman was dead.

The woman stirred. Her eyelids lifted a slit, and her fingers jerked. Sam crawled over to her. One whiff told her the woman hadn't had a bath for days. An undercurrent of something else reached her nose and set off warning bells in Sam's head.

"I'm Samantha Majors. I'm going to get you help."

The woman's hand reached for her, and her cracked lips moved. But nothing came out.

"Let me get you some water." Sam cast about the tent for a water bottle. "Here." She yanked one from the woman's backpack and opened it. Supporting her head, Sam helped her take a drink.

"Thank you." The woman, who could have been Mac, wrapped her fingers around Sam's wrist. "No help. No one must know where I am."

Her eyes burned into Sam's—one sapphire blue and one dark brown. Mac's eyes were both chestnut brown. Sam ran her flashlight over the woman's body and discovered the source of the unknown smell.

"But you're hurt." Coagulated blood covered the woman's shirt. "And I'm not equipped to help."

"You have a doctor in town who I trust. Doctor Hamilton." She dropped her hand and closed her eyes. "Please. Bring him to see me. I will pay you."

"Doc Hamilton retired, but we've got a whole hospital of doctors. And a new one moved in. He's good."

"No." Her answer was firm as her head lolled to one side.

"What happens now?" Mac bit her lip to keep it from trembling and glared at her captors.

"Now we leave." Scar Face pulled on his gloves.

"What about me?"

"Miss Love, my boss is an honorable man. He is not in the business of having people killed." Scar Face motioned to Cloudy Eye. "Get a bottled water and set it where she can reach it." He faced her again. "And we are not assassins. After we are well away, we will call the authorities and let them know where you are."

The two men gathered their things and took a last survey of the room. At the door, Scar Face looked at her once more. "I am sorry for the inconvenience we have caused you, but it couldn't be helped."

They pulled the door shut, and Mac heard a car engine start with a whine. Tires crunched on the rocky driveway. Then nothing.

She was alone.

Maybe they'd call the police—and maybe they wouldn't. From the brief time she'd had outside, she seemed to be in the middle of a forest. Screaming wouldn't help.

She examined the chair they tethered her to as best she could, running the fingers of her free hand over the armrest, searching for screws. None. She leaned against it. It didn't budge. Just her luck. Her chair was probably the sturdiest piece in this sparsely furnished house.

"Lord, I can't figure this out on my own, and I'm sure I don't have the strength." Mac lay her head on the table.

When she woke, the light through the windows had shifted. The shadows were longer. Mac ate a few bites of her stale sandwich and took a drink of water. Who knew how long she'd have to make this last?

She pressed harder against the arm of her chair. Anger

grew in her like wildfire. She roared and threw herself sideways against the offending arm. The chair crashed to the floor.

For a moment, pain numbed her, but the adrenaline coursing through her kept her moving. She used her body weight to roll the chair onto its back. Curling into a ball, she got her feet in a position to push on the armrest support.

And push she did. With all her might. Until with a mighty crack, the arm broke away from the chair. She was free.

"Thank you, Jesus." She lay back on the floor and covered her face with her hands as tears trickled down into her hair. Exhaustion replaced anger, and she wasn't sure her legs would support her. Maybe she would lay there awhile.

Tires sounded on the gravel drive. Mac jumped to her feet, heart pounding. Were they coming back? Had they changed their minds?

CHAPTER 17

Sam sat back on her heels and considered the woman before her. What should she do? An idea came to her. If only the woman would go along with it. "Wake up. I have an idea, but first tell me your name."

"Rosa," she murmured.

"Your full name."

"Rosa Lombardi."

"Okay, Rosa. Here's my plan." Sam sat on the floor of the tent next to her head. "I'll call my husband, who's a personal trainer, but also qualified as an EMT. If you're able, we'll move you to our house, which isn't far from here, where we'll take care of you until you're able to decide what to do next."

The woman shifted her head to face Sam, her eyes searching for any hint of deception. After a moment, she gave a slight nod. Sam knelt beside her. "I'll have to look at your injury in order to tell my husband what to expect."

She eased Rosa's shirt away from her wound. The odor of sickness wafted up, and she gulped to keep the bile from rising in her throat. On the woman's left side, a swollen three-inch slash oozed yellow liquid. The flesh surrounding the wound was red and angry. Sam glanced at Rosa. *This may be more than she and Alan could deal with.*

"How did you get this?"

"I was running and slipped. I fell on a sharp stone."

Sam stepped outside and dialed her husband. "I need your help."

About a half-hour later, Sam heard Alan calling her name. She grabbed Killer's harness and pulled him outside. "I hear daddy." She stooped by her dog and unhooked his leash. "Go find daddy."

The goldendoodle loped down the trail, stopped, and looked back at her. Alan shouted again. Killer's head whipped around toward the sound of his voice and took off. Sam sighed. For a moment, she thought her sweet dog wouldn't get the idea, but his poodle brain kicked in.

At least she hoped so. A lot could happen before Killer got to Alan. One squirrel and they might never see their dog again. Five minutes later, dog and master arrived at the campsite, and Sam gave her dog and her husband each a big hug.

Before entering the tent, she stopped Alan. "Brace yourself. You're not going to believe what you see."

"Sam, if it's bad, we shouldn't be messing with it. We need to get her to a hospital."

"It's not that. Rosa looks so much like Mac. It's scary." A shiver ran down her spine. "Except for the eyes."

Alan drew in a breath and let it out. "Okay. That I can deal with."

But when they entered the tent and Alan caught sight of Rosa on the cot, he stopped short, and Sam almost ran into him. "I told you," she whispered. She moved around him to kneel next to Mac's doppelgänger. "This is my husband, Alan."

She gave him a feeble wave.

Alan smiled and nodded. "First, I'm going to see what your wound looks like." He examined the gouge with a flashlight. "Not too bad. It needs cleaning. This will hurt. I'm sorry."

Sam offered the injured woman her hand, and as Alan worked on the gash, Rosa squeezed harder and harder.

"It's not as deep as I thought, but there's infection." Alan sat back on his heels. "Can you walk if I help you?"

"Yes."

"I'd like to take you to our place where we can keep it clean and take care of the infection." He went to the flaps covering the entrance to the tent and peered out. "We'll wait until dark."

"Thank you." Rosa lay back and closed her eyes. "You and Samantha have been very kind."

"We know you're in trouble, Rosa. But not why or from whom," Alan said.

Her eyes flew open.

"Our friend, Mackenzie Love, has been kidnapped because she looks like you."

A low moan escaped her lips. "Lord, have mercy on my soul. I never intended for anyone else to get hurt."

Tears sprang from Sam's eyes. Her heart was breaking for this woman and for her friend.

"Nobody ever does. You're running from something or someone. That's obvious."

Sam glared at Alan. How could he be so clinical with Rosa?

"We're going to need to know who or what in order to help Mac." He squatted where Rosa could look into his eyes. "And you. We need to know everything."

Rosa nodded.

"But first, we get you back to our house."

Voices and slamming car doors came from the front of the house. Mac's breath snagged in her throat. Were they back? Had they decided to kill her anyway? She grabbed a piece of the ruined chair and ran to a window. A police car sat behind a blue high-end sedan. She unlocked the door and yanked it open. The calvary had arrived at last.

"I'm here." She ran onto the porch. Two police officers rushed around the corner of the house, followed by Nate.

"Thank God." He gathered her into his arms. "I thought something terrible had happened to you."

She pushed him away. "What are you doing here?" Her hand tensed around the chair leg once more.

"I heard about your kidnapping on the police band radio at Aunt P's, and when they said you were somewhere in the Dittmer area, I rushed over to help search." He stepped toward her. "I drove past as the green van was leaving and called it in."

Another police car raced into the drive, sending gravel flying. Jake leaped out before the car came to a stop and ran to her. "Are you all right?" He pushed Nate out of the way and held her at arm's length. "Your cheek is bruised, and you've got cuts on your arms." He swung toward the officers. "Where are the paramedics?"

"They're on their way."

Jake put an arm around her waist. "Sit in my car until they get here. What's with the handcuffs?"

"It's a long story." She turned back to Nate. "Thank you. If you hadn't seen the van, it would have taken a lot longer for the police to find me."

"My pleasure." He gave her a little bow. "But it looks like you didn't need me after all."

"Be sure to let your aunt know I'm fine." What did he mean?

Nate tipped her a nod, got in his luxury sedan, and left.

"I still don't like the guy." Jake scowled after him. "Always sticking his nose in where it doesn't belong. He should have stayed home today."

Mac sat side-by-side with Jake in the back seat close enough for her to touch him. But she didn't. All she wanted was rest—and these handcuffs off her wrist.

"I, for one, am glad he came." She held up her arm. "Can you do something about these?"

"Hang on." Jake clicked a few photos. "We were close to finding you without wonder boy's help." He produced a key. "What's the story here, anyway?"

"They left me handcuffed to a chair, and I broke the chair."

He eyed her. "I have a feeling it wasn't as simple as you make it sound."

"I'll give you the longer version later. I'm exhausted."

"Okay." Jake put his phone in his pocket and got in the driver's seat. "We can go. Since the kidnapping took place in Washington, you'll give your statement to us. The police here will do forensics on the house." He caught her eye in the rearview mirror. "Buckle up."

"Yes, sir." She strapped in, leaned against the window, and closed her eyes.

Nate's words tumbled over in her mind. *Looks like you didn't need me after all.* Not the words so much, but something about his tone.

She'd think about it later, after she slept.

CHAPTER 18

"I'm going home to get the room ready." Sam pushed to her feet. "I'll be back soon."

Alan followed Sam out of the tent. "Take Killer with you so I don't have to keep track of him." He brushed hair away from Sam's face. "Be careful."

"You too." She planted a light kiss on his lips. "Come on, Killer. Let's go home."

When Sam got to the backyard, it surprised her how light it still was. Amongst the trees, it seemed much later in the day. The room they called the office would be Rosa's sick room. Besides a desk, the room held a daybed, small table, and an armchair. Sam vacuumed, made the bed, and cleared the table.

Before heading back, she put a casserole in the oven on the timer. The poor woman had had little to eat for days, and it would be nice to come home to a house filled with the aroma of good food.

"Okay, dog. Time to go back." Sam snatched a flashlight from a kitchen drawer and headed out the door.

The sun had set, and the woods behind her house were in

deep shadow. Sam clicked her light on. Killer ran ahead. Her calming forest had become a different place and the line "Lions and tigers and bears! Oh, my!" kept running through her head. She quickened her pace.

In the distance, Killer barked, and two gunshots echoed off the trees. Alan. Sam ran toward the sound, her heart in her throat. A flickering light shone through the brush. The camp. Sam burst into the small clearing.

A small fire threw light on her precious husband's face down on the ground, sticks cast around him. Killer crouched by his side and whined. Sam dropped to her knees.

"Alan. God no. Please."

He stirred and grunted.

Sam swiped the tears from her eyes. "Alan, can you hear me? Are you all right? Did they shoot you?"

"Yes. No. Yes." His feeble reply sounded through gritted teeth. "In my leg."

"Oh, baby." Sam hovered over him. "What can I do?"

"Check on Rosa and call 911."

Sam sat up with a jolt. Rosa. Two shots. She pushed into the tent and crawled to the cot. The pale woman struggled for breath. Blood seeped between her fingers, pressed to her chest.

"I've called for help." Sam found gauze and, lifting Rosa's hands, applied pressure herself.

"Your husband?" Rosa whispered.

"Shot in the leg. He'll be fine." Sam prayed she spoke the truth.

"I told him ... everything."

"Don't talk. Relax and save your energy." The bleeding seemed to have slowed. Sam hoped it was a good sign. She looked at Rosa, who appeared to be resting. Where were those paramedics?

Alan dragged himself half inside the tent. "I heard a siren. They should be here soon. How's she doing?"

"She's resting, and the bleeding has slowed."

"See if you can wake her."

"Rosa?" Sam touched her face. It was cool. "Rosa?" She shook her. The woman's eyelids fluttered. "Stay with us. Help is almost here."

Killer's frenzied barking alerted them to the men. Alan silenced the dog as two EMTs rushed into the campsite. One stayed with Alan, while the other joined Sam by Rosa's side.

"We're going to need another bus," one man said into his shoulder mic.

Two police officers stood outside. Sam trudged over to them. "I'm Samantha Majors. Detective Jake Sanders is my brother. He's not answering my calls. Can you let him know what's going on?"

"Of course, Mrs. Majors."

She turned and marched back to her husband. "I'll meet you at the hospital."

"I'm not going. It's a flesh wound."

Sam looked at the EMTs. "Would you give us a moment?" They backed off a couple of feet.

"Alan." She came in close. "What would you say if it were me?"

He avoided her eyes. "This is different."

"How?"

"I'm a man, and you're a woman."

She stiffened. "We've had this discussion before. We agreed never to use that excuse. Remember?"

He looked at her. "I hate hospitals."

"Nobody likes hospitals. But I'm asking you to do this. I love you, and I want to know you're okay."

He pushed a hand through her hair to the back of her head and drew her in for a kiss. "I'll go."

She motioned for the EMTs to come back. "I'll take Killer home and meet you at the hospital. I love you."

"Love you more."

JAKE ACTED LIKE A JERK, while Nate behaved like a gentleman. Nobody told him who made the 911 call, and he hadn't expected to see Mac's old boyfriend at the scene. Still, he should have been nicer to Nate. He glanced in the rearview mirror at Mackenzie. He wouldn't blame Mac if she didn't want to have anything to do with him.

His phone lit up. "This is Detective Sanders." Jake pushed a button on his steering wheel for his hands-free phone.

"Detective, we have a message from your sister, Mrs. Majors." A sneeze echoed through the receiver. "Sorry."

Jake glanced in the rearview mirror. Mac nestled in the corner, eyes closed. Good. He turned the volume down. "Go ahead."

"She wanted you to know her husband's been shot and is at the hospital."

"Alan's been shot? What happened? Is Sam okay?" Mac's strident voice sounded over his shoulder.

He motioned for her to be quiet.

"Pardon me, sir? I didn't get that. I'm allergic to leaves and—"

"I understand. Is that all she said in her message?"

"Well, she said to tell you what happened, but it would take too long. We figured you could call her and find out the rest for yourself?"

"Is Alan's injury life-threatening?"

"Oh, no, sir. He got shot in the leg. He'll be fine. And your sister and her dog are fine, too." Another sneeze. "The other woman is in pretty bad shape. The doc's not sure if she'll pull through."

"The other woman?" Jake gripped the steering wheel to keep from yelling. "What other woman?"

"Rosa Lombardi. Sounds Italian to me."

"Where did the shootings take place?"

"In the woods behind your sister's house."

Jake shared a mystified look with Mac before thanking the officer and ending the call.

"Buckle up," Jake said as he hit the lights and siren.

CHAPTER 19

No sooner did he rescue one woman in his life than another one ended up in the middle of trouble. He'd say it was like herding cats, except his cat was better behaved. Jake swung into a parking space at the hospital and jumped out of the car.

"Come on, Mac. You need to be checked out by a doc." He held out a hand to help her out of the backseat.

She ignored his hand. "I told you. I'm fine."

"Don't be hardheaded." His tone sounded harsher than he intended.

"Okay." Mac lifted her hands in surrender.

He'd caught the look of hurt on her face, and a flash of guilt traveled through him. He turned and led the way to the emergency room door. At the door, he let Mac enter ahead of him.

"Sir." An officer hurried over to Jake. "Your brother-in-law is in room five. Your sister's with him."

"Thanks." Jake walked to the information desk. "I've got a kidnap victim who needs attention."

"You guys are bringing us lots of work tonight." The nurse studied her screen. "Take her to room three."

"Thanks." Jake escorted Mac through the double doors and down the hall to room three. "Can you wait here for the doc on your own? I'd like to see how Alan's doing."

"I'm a big girl. I can take care of myself."

"What's the matter, Mac?" But he had a good idea what the answer would be, and regret sat like a stone in his stomach.

"Nothing." She waved him away. "Go."

Nothing was wrong with her—except a bruised heart. Mac swiped tears away as the door opened on a young doctor.

"It says here you were a kidnap victim?"

The compassion in his eyes ruptured her resolve, and she sobbed. He placed an arm around her shoulder and let her blubber all over his clean white jacket.

"I'm sorry." Her breathing hitched as she spoke. "I'm not usually like this."

He handed her a box of tissues. "I think surviving being kidnapped entitles you to at least one good cry. Now, let's see about your other injuries."

"I don't feel bad. Just exhausted."

"We'll take a urine sample and blood to look for evidence of internal injuries. Your cuts don't need stitches, and your bruises aren't deep." He examined her eyes. "Headaches?"

"No."

"Good. You're very lucky, Miss Love." He smiled at her. "Wait here. The nurse will be in to take care of the rest."

"Thanks, doctor." At least she was doing something about her body, but what could she do about her heart?

Jake treated her like a friend—no, less than a friend, like an irritating acquaintance. And it was tearing her apart.

And there were Alan and Sam. She ached to go to her friends, but should she? Jake was with them, and she wasn't sure she wanted to be around him right now. The door opened, and a nurse entered the room.

"I'm here to take your blood," she said in a Count Dracula voice.

Mac held out her arm and winced at the prick of the needle.

The nurse finished drawing her blood, wrapped the cotton ball in place, and handed her a cup. "The bathroom's across the hall. You know what to do."

When Mac got back to her room, Jake was waiting there. She averted her gaze and took a step toward the bed.

He blocked her way. "It seems all I do these days is mess up with you." He raised a hand as if to stroke her cheek and let it drop. "I'm sorry."

Mac glared. "For what? Bossing me around or treating me like nothing but trouble in your life?"

"Both."

She tore her gaze from his pleading blue eyes. "This has to stop. You can't keep being ugly to me and apologizing later."

"You're right." He grasped her waist and pulled her toward him.

"I can't do this now," she whispered as she placed her hands on his chest.

"Good news." The door swung open, and the young doctor breezed in. "Oh. Sorry."

Mac and Jake broke apart.

"Doctor, come in," she said.

He glanced from Mac to Jake and back to Mac. "You're free

to go. Your tests results came back good." He paused at the door. "Take care of her, Detective."

"I'll do my best." Jake put a hand out to stop him. "Are you treating the shooting victim who came in earlier?"

"Which one? The man or the woman?"

"The woman."

"No." He flipped a page on his clipboard. "She's in surgery. Her file says she lost a lot of blood." His young face aged before her eyes. "She may not make it. I'm sorry."

"Thanks, doc," Jake said.

When they were alone, Mac advanced on Jake. "Who is this mysterious woman?"

"Come on. I'll let Sam tell you." Jake held the door for her and led the way down the hall to Alan's room.

Sam intercepted them coming in and waved them out of the room. "The doctor's sewing up Alan's leg." She threw her arms around Mac. "Thank God you're okay. I don't know what I'd do if something happened to you too. My heart can only take so much."

"Thank God we're all okay." Sam's embrace warmed Mac's soul. "And it sounds like we've both got stories to tell."

"Yes." Sam held her at arm's length. "We found your doppelwhatsit and—"

"Wait." Jake interrupted. "Are you saying the woman who's been shot is Mac's look-alike?"

"Yes, and she told Alan all about it."

"What did she tell him?" An icy finger ran down Mac's spine.

"I'm not sure. He and I haven't had a chance to talk." Sam put a hand to her throat. "But before she passed out, Rosa said she told Alan everything."

The doctor and nurse came out of Alan's room and stopped next to Sam. "Your husband is resting now. We gave him a mild sedative before stitching his wound. It may take a while to wear off."

"How bad was it?" Jake asked.

"The bullet grazed the fleshy part of your friend's outer thigh. He'll be sore but should be fine in a week." He glanced at his charts. "I've left instructions on how to care for the wound and any restrictions on the table next to his bed. He can leave as soon as he wakes."

"Thank you, doctor," Sam said.

"I can drive you guys and Mac home," Jake said.

"No need." Mackenzie zipped her coat. "I called Miss P to come pick me up, and she's offered to stay with me tonight."

"And I drove here behind the ambulance," Sam said. "I can take Alan home."

"Oh." Concern pinched Jake's forehead in the middle. "I'll follow you home, Mac, to make sure you're okay."

"We'll be fine. Thanks." She fiddled with the clasp on her purse.

Jake shuffled his feet and glanced at her. "Mac, I'm—"

"When's your mom getting back from her retreat?" Mac asked.

"Tomorrow afternoon." Sam peeked in the door to Alan's room. "He's waking up."

The friends helped Sam get Alan to her car at the emergency room door and waved goodbye. Mac peered into the darkness. Where was Miss P? The familiar scent of Jake's aftershave brought an intense physical awareness of his presence. Her heart drummed in her chest.

"Mac, I know I come off as controlling and like I'm irritated with you." He moved closer. "But the truth is, I'm scared. Scared you'll get hurt or worse. I can't handle it." He touched her hair. "Pretty selfish. I know."

She turned to face him. "You're a police officer. If we are to have a relationship, you would expect me to handle you going to work every day—putting yourself in harm's way—and not only deal with it but be a caring and loving girlfriend to you. Why shouldn't I be able to expect the same?"

"You should." His intense gaze bore into her. "I'm not sure I can, but I'm working on it."

"Our relationship depends on it, Jake. I should be able to do my job and rely on you to support me with love and compassion."

"I get it."

"Miss Love?" A nurse hurried through the emergency doors. "I'm so glad I caught you. You left this in the room." She held out the cross necklace torn from Mac's neck in the green van.

As the delicate chain pooled in Mac's palm, her blood froze. The last time she'd seen her cross had been in her kidnapper's van where it had been ripped from her neck. Who ...? She shivered as she probed the parking lot for a dark green van.

CHAPTER 20

After another restless sleep, Mac arrived at the office with more questions than answers. She pulled a chair out at the head of the table. A steaming cup of coffee sat at her right hand next to a fresh yellow notepad and sharpened pencil. She touched the cross necklace at her throat—once more where it belonged. She was ready.

"Sam should be here soon." Miss P took a seat to her left. "Her mother has graciously offered to sit with Alan today. Although I gather he insisted he could—and should—join us."

"She's going to have her hands full." Mac barked a laugh. "He's as strong willed as Sam is."

"Indeed."

"Good morning." The door opened to the office, and Sam breezed in. "I brought a friend." Alan stepped over the threshold, leaning on a cane. He made his way to the table, his mouth set in a determined line.

Mac and Miss P shared an I-told-you-so look. Miss P jumped up to get him a cup of coffee.

"As good as it is to see you, Alan, you should be home resting," Mac said.

"Save your breath." Sam got her husband settled and sat next to him. "It's like talking to a teenager."

"I'm fine." Alan cast a scowl at his wife. "I know what I can and can't do."

"Yes, dear."

"You guys need to hear what Rosa told me firsthand." A muscle in his jaw twitched. "Especially you, Mac."

His words brought up the hairs on the back of her neck. "Why me?"

"Because you look like her, and she's in real danger."

Jake pushed through the door and marched across the room. "Sorry. I was arranging police protection for Rosa Lombardi."

"How is she?" Sam asked.

"She survived the surgery, but the next couple of days will tell whether she makes it." Jake scuffed a hand through his hair. "She's in an induced coma."

"It sounds like there's no time to lose. We need to get to work." Mac pressed her lips together in a grim line. "First, I'll summarize my story." She began with the kidnapping and took them through how she escaped and was recaptured. "But every time I expected them to rough me up, they held back. The one with the cloudy eye wanted to, but he never did."

"Did he tell you why?"

"All along, they kept saying my father was trying to protect me—which we now know would be Rosa's father. I didn't believe them. At the end, I was sure they were going to shoot me after they found out I wasn't who they thought." Mac touched the cross at her neck once more. "They said their boss wasn't in the business of killing people and they weren't assassins."

"They handcuffed you to a chair and left?" Sam sounded mystified.

"Yes." Mac said in a soft voice. "They promised to call the police once they were safe, and I believe they would have if Nate hadn't seen them leave."

"They did," Jake said. "Four hours after we found you, an anonymous call came in to the local police station."

"Were you able to trace it?"

Jake shook his head.

"In the meantime, Sam, you took a walk in the woods." Mac raised an eyebrow at her friend.

"I was worried about you. I couldn't sit in the house waiting for word."

"I get it, my friend. I would have been a basket case if it had been you." Mac tossed her a grin. "I bet you didn't expect to find me laying on a cot in the woods though."

"It was a real shock." Sam leaned back in her chair. "I screamed, and Killer barged in to protect me." She chuckled. "I always wondered if he'd come to my rescue or run away. Now we know."

"We sure do," Alan said. "When the guy with the gun showed up, Killer jumped him as he was coming out of the tent and ruined his aim. I came here today to tell my part of the story."

"What happened that night?" Jake asked.

"I went for wood," Alan said. "I was almost back when I heard a gunshot. The guy must have heard me coming and stepped out of the tent. He aimed at me, and then Killer arrived. He launched himself at the man as the gun fired."

"Thank God for your dog." Jake leaned forward. "I'm sure the man would have killed you and gone back into the tent to finish Miss Lombardi off."

"So, Killer saved two people." Sam sighed. "If Rosa lives."

"Did anyone take samples from Killer's nails and teeth?" Jake asked.

"I don't remember them doing that." Sam looked at Alan. "Of course, we were busy making sure Alan and Rosa were taken care of."

"It's probably too late now, but I'll send someone round your house to do the tests." Jake pulled his phone from his pocket. "Can't be used in court, but it could point us to a suspect."

"I'll tell Mom to expect them." Sam rose and went into her office.

Mac scratched notes on her pad. This was the part she enjoyed most—brainstorming about a case with her friends and colleagues. But, once again, she and Sam found themselves on a case with no promise of payment at the end. It was a miracle they'd made it as long as they had and turned a profit.

No matter. Each case was of equal importance to them. And this one involved her in a very personal way. She didn't like to think someone out there might shoot her by accident. The very idea made her skin itch as if eyes were watching her right now. She glanced at the windows. Time to get curtains for their office building. Thick ones.

Miss P poured fresh coffee for everyone and sat back down. "Mr. Masters, I, for one, would like to hear what Miss Lombardi related to you before being shot."

"Yes." Mac focused again on Alan. "What she told you may hold the key to who's behind all this."

"Don't start without me." Sam breezed through the room, headed for the bathroom. "I'll be right back."

"Hurry, sis." Jake called after her.

"Okay." Sam returned a few minutes later and yanked her chair out. "I'm back."

"Take a breath." Alan placed a hand on hers. "We've got time."

A flash of clarity hit Mac. She wanted what Sam and Alan had. Love. Respect. Concern. Joy. She slid her eyes to Jake. Could she have those things with him? That remained a mystery still to be solved. For now, she needed to focus on what Alan was saying about Rosa.

"...about six months ago and she's been hiding out since."

"I'm sorry, Alan. Did you say Rosa left home six months ago?"

"Yeah. She met a man she fell hard for, and they got married. But she realized it was a big mistake." He pressed his lips together. "Her father is a successful businessman in Chicago, and he put the majority of his stock in his wife's name."

"For the tax breaks?" Jake asked.

"I guess. When his wife died, she left her stock to their daughter, Rosa."

"And Rosa's husband is after a controlling interest in her father's company."

"Only if Rosa dies." Mac shivered.

"Or divorces him, which is what she's in the process of doing. That and changing her will," Alan said. "The reason she came to Washington."

"Why here?"

"Mr. Fischer is her godfather. He and his wife were old friends of her mother's. Rosa wanted his help with the new will. I didn't understand how she expected him to help her."

"Had she contacted him?" Was his problem connected with Rosa?

"No." Alan picked up his mug. "She hurt herself before she could get to him."

"What about the husband?" Jake asked. "Any description?"

"She'd gotten to the point of telling me about her husband when I stopped her." Alan's face fell. "I needed to get wood before it got too dark. I thought we'd have time to talk later."

Sam wrapped an arm around her husband's shoulders. "You had no way of knowing, sweetheart."

"Sam's right," Jake said. "Don't blame yourself for what happened. She told you enough. We can get the rest."

"I think it's time to call Mr. Fischer." Mac pressed numbers on her phone.

"And I'll order pizzas for lunch," Miss P said.

CHAPTER 21

Jake worked hard to keep his face relaxed. He hadn't seen Mr. Fischer for several months, and the man seemed to have aged years. Gone was the perfectly groomed businessman. Instead, this man needed a haircut. His shirt gaped at his neck, and he shuffled when he walked.

But Mr. Fischer spoke, and Jake relaxed.

"Don't be fooled by my appearance, young man." Mr. Fischer fixed Jake with a gleeful look. "It's a ruse meant to make my enemies think I'm weak."

"Yes, sir." What enemies was he trying to trick? And why?

"Thanks for coming, Mr. Fischer." Mac handed him a glass of tea. "Would you like some pizza?"

"No, thanks."

"Something's come up, and we could use your help."

"I am at your disposal." He looked around the table at each of them. "Although I must admit, I'm curious as to what can involve so many of you."

"We've each had a part in ... I'm not sure what to call it," Mac said. "It's not a case, although we're searching for an answer, so I guess that's what we'll call it. The case of mistaken identity."

The old man gave a slow nod.

"We were told you and your wife were friends with Rosa Lombardi's mother. Were you?"

"Yes." A sad smile touched his lips. "A lovely woman."

"When did you last see her?" Jake studied Fischer's face.

"I attended her funeral ten years ago."

"How close are you to her daughter, Rosa?"

Fischer's brow creased. "She came to visit with her mother when she was young, and I saw her briefly at her mother's funeral, but that's the extent of our involvement with each other. Why do you ask, Detective?"

"You haven't seen or heard from her since?"

"I told you, no." He leaned back in his chair. "Why are you questioning me about Rosa and her mother?"

"Because Rosa's in the hospital here in Washington. She's been shot."

"Oh, no." His eyes widened. "I must go to her."

The man looked stricken. Were the enemies Fischer mentioned the same ones who shot Rosa?

"I'm sorry." Jake softened his tone. "No one can see her. She's in a coma and under police protection."

"What has she done?"

"According to what she told Alan, she married a man who's only interested in her father's company."

"Like her mother." Fischer placed his head in his hands.

"What do you mean?"

"The company Rosa's father runs belonged to her mother's family. Her mother owned most of the stock, and she passed it to their daughter when she died."

"So, you're saying Rosa's father married her mother to get

control of her grandfather's company?" Tears rimmed Sam's eyes.

Mr. Fischer nodded.

"And the same thing's happening to Rosa, but she doesn't have a will leaving it to her daughter. If she had a daughter."

A heavy silence descended on the table.

"That's why she came here." Mac looked at Mr. Fischer. "She wanted your help to draw up a will."

"There's still time." Mr. Fischer straightened. "You said she's in a coma. I will begin on the will today."

"Before you take off, we've got a few more questions for you." Jake consulted his notes. "I need photos of Rosa's husband."

"I heard something about Rosa getting married, but they did not invite me. It must have been a private affair, but I saw no photos. Rosa's father avoids publicity."

"Weird." Sam retrieved her computer and started typing.

"Do you think your fall could be someone trying to stop you from connecting with Rosa?" Mac asked.

"As I said, my fall turned out to be an unfortunate accident." Mr. Fischer waved a dismissive hand in the air. "Our maintenance man sat a pot of glue on the steps, intending to repair some loose tiles. He got called away and forgot about it. Someone must have knocked it over, and the glue spilled on the steps." Fischer ran a hand over his forehead. "When he realized what had happened, he cleaned it up and said nothing because he felt terrible about my fall. Especially since he's usually so good about screwing the lid on the pot."

"How did you find out?" Jake asked.

"His conscience got the better of him, and he came to me the other day."

Mac raised an eyebrow in disbelief. She hadn't noticed any loose tiles on the stairs. "How long has this maintenance man worked for you?"

"I'm not sure. Human Resources would know."

She glanced around the room. Alan's pale face snagged her attention. "Sam, I think your husband needs a break."

"Yep." Her partner pushed back from the table. "Come on, macho man, time to go."

"I want to stay. I've got a stake in this case."

"But you're no good to us unless you take care of yourself." Mac rose. "Come on."

"I've got something you can help with at home." Sam helped him to his feet and handed him his cane. "While I search the web for Rosa's mysterious husband, you can read through Mac's old college newspapers."

"Why?"

"I'll tell you on the way." Sam waved goodbye and escorted her husband out the door.

"I should go as well." Mr. Fischer scooted forward on his chair.

"Before you leave, any strange happenings at the factory in the past few days?" Mac sat and pulled her notebook in front of her.

"Unfortunately, yes." He let out a heavy sigh. "My desk drawer wasn't shut all the way this morning when I came in, and I've been very careful about locking my desk as of late. At least twice a week people come to me complaining about things being out of place or moved."

"Do you think it might be someone playing practical jokes?" Miss P asked.

"It doesn't have the feeling of a prankster. It's more like someone snooping around, but I can't imagine why. Unless ..."

"Unless what?" Mac raised her head to peer at him.

He studied his hands for a long moment. "I'm not supposed to say anything to anyone. But these curious incidents began happening soon after Fischer Industries put a bid on a job for Boeing Aeronautical in St. Louis."

"So they could be related to your prospective job?"

"I can't help wondering if I have an industrial spy working at Fischer Industries. Someone who is either gathering information in an attempt to out-bid us, or to sabotage us if we are awarded the contract." He pushed his bottom lip forward in thought. "I suppose that's why I initially felt something or someone had tripped me."

CHAPTER 22

"I'm not convinced you weren't." Mac stood as Fischer struggled to his feet, leaning hard on the table. "But we'll let that go for now. I'll see you to your car."

Back inside the office, Mac closed the door and stood with her hand on the knob a moment longer. "I've been thinking."

"Always a dangerous thing," Jake said.

"Hah, hah." Mac crossed to the table and sat. "We need to make a list of people who are new to the area. I have a feeling Rosa's husband expected her trying to reach Mr. Fischer, and he sent someone here undercover."

"Okay." Jake pulled out a chair. "I get it."

"I can see where such a list would be helpful," Miss P said. "I suppose we should start with my nephew."

"Thanks, Miss P. I hated to be the one to say it." Mac wrote Nate's name down.

"Add the new doctor, David Quinn." Jake tapped the table.

"And we should contact Human Resources at Fischer Industries to see who the new hires have been within the past year or so." Miss P made a note. "I'll compile the list tomorrow."

"One will be Claudia Smith, Mr. Fischer's new assistant." Mac studied her list. "And be sure to ask about the maintenance man. I'll set up a lunch with Ivy and see what I can find out about her boyfriend, the doctor."

"I'll run background checks. Send me names when you get them." Jake pushed to his feet. "Anything else?"

"Yes." Mac hesitated. "I'd like to see Rosa." Her heart pounded in her chest.

"Are you sure about that?"

She nodded. But was she?

"Okay. I'll meet you at the hospital in the morning." Jake moved next to her and brushed her cheek with the back of his hand. "See you tomorrow."

Shafts of electricity coursed through her veins, followed by frustration. Why did she let this man get to her? "Tomorrow." She kept her eyes on her notepad until she heard the door close.

"Mackenzie, I'll clean up the mess if you will take the bags to the garbage." Miss P stacked paper plates and headed for the kitchen. "I'm meeting friends for dinner tonight."

"No problem." Mac grabbed the napkins and followed her. "I may stay at the office for a while."

"Please be careful." Miss P kissed her on the cheek. "I don't think you realize how special you are to the people around you. Including me."

Mac swallowed the sudden lump of emotion. "I feel the same about you." A flash of realization hit her. "Where's Nate been today?"

"He said he had work to do." The older woman shrugged. "I suppose he has a new case."

Interesting. Mac hadn't heard of anything requiring a

lawyer in the area. She tied off the white bag and headed for the back door.

As she lifted the lid on the trashcan, a shiver ran down her spine. Bits and pieces from a night like this flitted through her mind. Sam at the back door. Two men in black. Pain. The scene shifted, and she was in the car again. Her sister, Beth, screamed as they lurched to the right.

Mac pressed her back to the side of the house, unable to move.

"Mackenzie?" Miss P laid a gentle hand on her shoulder.

Mac jerked and cocked her arm to deliver a punch.

Miss P screamed and threw her arms up to cover her face.

"Oh, dear." Mac dropped her arms. "Miss P, I'm so sorry."

"It's all right, my dear." Miss P held out her hand. "Let's go inside."

"You know I didn't mean to hurt you."

"I know, but Sam told me about the incident in the hospital. She believes you should see someone, and I agree," Miss P said. "I may be speaking out of bounds, but you and Sam have become like the daughters I never had."

Love poured from Miss P's eyes straight into Mac's heart. Since the death of her parents, Mac let herself get close enough to people to care, but not so close she'd be ripped apart if they left.

For the first time, Mac realized the people she cared about had let her into their hearts. They didn't have barriers and were willing to take the chance on being torn to shreds. Maybe it was time she did the same for them.

"I promise I will." She took Miss P's hand in hers.

"Good." A satisfied smile lit up Miss P's face. "Now I must go. Don't stay much longer. You need sleep." At the door, she turned. "And be careful."

"Yes, mother." Mac grinned at her friend.

After securing the door, Mac dropped into an armchair in the reception area. She'd keep her promise to Miss P and see a doctor about her episodes, but she had no idea who. She stared at her phone for a long time before pressing the button. With every ring, her heart rate increased. Would her sister want to talk to her about that time?

"Mac, what's up?" Her oldest sister's voice sounded in her ear.

"Hi, Beth. You got a minute?"

"Sure, sweetheart. What's wrong?"

Beth had picked up the quake in Mac's voice and became the protective big sister Mac remembered from their childhood. Tears pricked the back of her eyes.

"I need your help." Mac related the incidents with the nurse, the balloon popping, and outside at the trashcan. "Sam and Miss P want me to see a doctor ... and I agree with them."

"Oh, Mackenzie. I'm glad you agree," Beth said. "You know what I went through when Mom and Dad died. I waited too long to get help."

"That's why I called you. I want the name of your doctor."

"I'll text you the name of my doctor, but it was a long time ago. I can't guarantee he's still in practice."

Mac hesitated. "And I want to talk to you about when Mom and Dad died. I'm getting visions I can't explain."

Silence. Had she lost the connection?

"Beth, are you still there?"

"I'm here." She sighed. "It's time you know the whole story, but not until we can meet face-to-face. Maybe at Thanksgiving."

"Tell me this. Is it bad?"

"Only if you consider the truth bad. I have to go. Let me know if you get an appointment."

Mac checked the windows and the back door, flipping

lights off as she went. Everything was back in place after the party. The chairs and couch in the reception area sat a right angle with pillows plumped. The polished conference table gleamed with the chairs placed at regular intervals.

From the outside, her life looked organized and in control. But inside, everything in her life floated above her head, just out of her grasp. She needed sleep.

THE MORNING AIR HAD WARMED, and fog clung to the trees. Indian summer, Mac's mom called it. It wouldn't last, but for now, it suited her mood. Out of sorts. She sat by her front window and sipped her second cup of coffee.

She'd dreamed of fighting with helium balloons again. Except this time, one had Rosa's face on it, another Jake's, a third Nate's, a fourth Mr. Fischer's face, and the last one contained a shadowy visage she kept trying to pull closer. It didn't take a genius to figure out that imagery.

In the dream, she was having so much trouble hanging onto the balloons she didn't see the man approach her. It was the shadowy man, and he had a gun. This time, he shot at her. She woke before the bullet hit her.

The verse about casting all cares on God ran through her mind, and she knew what she had to do. Time to put her troubles with Jake and Nate aside and concentrate on Rosa and Mr. Fischer. She imagined letting go of Jake's and Nate's balloons. The others shrunk to a manageable size, and relief flooded through her.

Her troubled sleep left her groggy, and she forgot about her request to see Rosa. She headed for her office. Once she remembered, she took a roundabout route. Instead of turning right off Hill Street onto Fifth and heading directly to the hospital, she traveled along Second before hopping up to Fifth via Burnside.

Jake had agreed to meet her at nine o'clock, and it was five till. She was going to be late. She hated being late. Her phone rang.

"I'm running late," Jake said. "Be there in ten."

"No problem." She smiled to herself and pulled into the hospital parking lot. *Thank you, Jesus.*

As Jake drove in, she finished her coffee and threw the container into the trash. He hurried across the lot.

"Sorry. I try to be on time."

"It's okay. It gave me time to drink my coffee."

He eyed her. "Sure you want to do this? I can tell you from experience it's a shock."

"I'm ready."

They took the elevator to the second floor. At Rosa's door, the officer stood.

"Detective Sanders and Private Investigator Mackenzie Love."

The officer stared at Mac. "Yes, sir."

"Write it down, man."

"Yes, sir." The man scribbled their names on a sheet.

Jake opened the door. Mac took a deep breath. Was she ready for whoever lay on the bed through that door? Maybe. Maybe not. But she had to know.

CHAPTER 23

Mac hesitated a couple feet from the bed. The only body part visible on the still shapeless bulge under the blankets was a slender white arm. Mac's heartbeat pounded in her ears. She stepped closer.

The lights were dim, and a nest of tubes and wires surrounded the woman's body. She walked to the side of the bed and looked down.

On herself.

The room seemed to spin. Her knees buckled. Strong arms caught her. A chair pushed under her.

"I told you." Jake squatted before her, lines of concern etched on his face. "Drink." He handed her a glass of water.

She took a sip and glanced at the still form in the bed. Was this glass meant for her?

"It's not hers."

Mac snapped her eyes back to Jake. How had he known what she was thinking?

"I know you." He brushed hair away from her eyes.

"She could be my twin." Her voice came as a whisper.

Jake nodded. "Except she has one blue eye and one brown eye."

"But her features and her hair." Mac raised a hand to her head.

"Yes."

"I guess I thought I would see her differently. I thought I'd look at her and not see the resemblance." She shuddered. "It's spooky."

"Now you understand why you were attacked in the first place. They—whoever they are—tracked Rosa as far as Washington, and when they saw you ..."

"That part makes sense." Mac glanced at the woman in the bed. "But why run away from her father? And to Mr. Fischer? When they held me captive, they made it sound as if her father wanted to protect her, not hurt her. And they didn't hurt me."

"I don't have the answers." Jake stood. "Yet. But we will."

Mac rose and walked over to the bed once more.

"The nurse told me she can hear what we say to her, even in a coma," Jake said.

"Rosa, I'm Mackenzie Love. When you wake up, we've got a lot to talk about. We could pass for twins. They tell me the only difference is our eyes." Mac paused. "I ... pray you get better soon, so we get a chance to know each other."

The door opened, and a man hunched over an industrial dust mop walked in. "Come to clean the room."

"Do you want us to leave?" Mac asked.

He shook his head.

The man struggled to steer the big mop around the room. It was clear he hadn't been doing this for long. Something about him niggled at her. Dark hair slicked back away from an olive-toned face with a Roman nose.

As he let the door close behind him, he glanced at her with cold gray eyes. Unease rolled through her like a chilled, dark wave. She shook it off. Every guy she didn't know seemed suspicious to her right now. She was being paranoid.

"Let's go." Jake took her arm.

In the hall, Mac stopped a nurse. "How is she?"

The professional woman glanced at Jake, who nodded consent.

"We're doing everything we can, but her wound was significant."

"Thank you." A heaviness settled in Mac's chest.

"Are you her sister?"

"No. I'm helping find who shot her."

"You look ... well, anyway. We'll take good care of her."

"I'm sure you will." Mac joined Jake. "Let's get out of here."

PART OF MAC'S mind signaled her feet to brake at stoplights and to her hands to make the turns, while the other part stood by Rosa's bed and gazed at the woman who could be her twin. She prayed Rosa would wake up because she had a lot of questions for her. What were her favorite foods? Her favorite books? Did she lose her temper as easily as Mac did?

Did she ever need help?

Mac pulled into the driveway at her office, but had no recollection of the journey. The smell of fresh brewed coffee greeted her as she entered the office building, and she headed for the kitchen.

"Good morning, Mackenzie." Miss P held out a mug for her.

"Thanks." She took the cup and headed for her office.

"Mac." Sam called through her open door. "How was your trip to the hospital this morning?"

She stopped outside Sam's doorway. "It was pretty freaky

at first. I guess I hadn't expected Rosa to look so much like me. If that makes any sense."

"I get it." Sam raised her eyes from the computer screen. "How are you?"

"I'm fine." Mac drew in a breath and let it out. She took inventory. "Yeah. I'm fine."

"Good." Sam threw her a smile. "I haven't had any luck with Rosa's husband yet. Talk about strange."

"Nowadays, that's beyond strange. But if anyone can dig it out, it'll be you." Mac gestured toward her office. "I'll be in there for a while, and then I'm having lunch with Ivy to get the scoop on her doctor."

"And I'm going to Fischer Industries to speak with their head of Human Resources," Miss P said.

"Let's meet back here this afternoon to compare notes." Mac took a sip of coffee and moved away.

Miss P followed her into her office. "Mackenzie, I know it's none of my business, but I'm making it my business. Do you need help finding a doctor?"

"No, Miss P." Mac sat her mug on the desk. "I talked to my sister last night and got the name of the guy she saw. I'll call him today." She hugged Miss P. "Thank you for caring enough to make it your business."

"I told you last night how I feel." She stepped back. "Now get to work, and we'll talk again later."

Mac sat for a moment. She sipped her coffee before picking up her phone and dialing the doctor's office number Beth gave her. After explaining her problem, she got an appointment for two weeks from tomorrow. A knot deep in her chest unraveled.

"I'm headed home to have lunch with Alan." Sam bobbed into Mac's office. "Aren't you supposed to be having lunch with Ivy?"

"What time is it?" Mac jumped up. Was she late again?

"Eleven-thirty."

"We're meeting at noon." She'd make it on time.

They'd decided to eat somewhere other than Cowan's. Ivy worked there, and she needed a change. She'd gotten reservations at The Nest Cafe, the elegant two-story brick house on Elm, with its antique furnishings and amazing gift shop.

When the weather was nice, Mac loved to sit out on the shaded patio, but not today. A November wind ran icy fingers across her face and through her hair, reminding her winter was just around the corner. Inside, honey-toned wood and the heavenly smells of fresh bread and hot soup combined to warm her spirit if not her body.

Ivy waved to her from a table in the corner by a graceful, tall bookcase with a glass door.

"Have you ordered yet?" Mac removed her coat and draped it over a spare chair.

"No, I waited for you." Ivy raised and lowered her shoulders in excitement, a big smile on her face. "Isn't this place great?"

"It's one of my favorites."

"I don't get to come here much, but since I've been dating David, I eat at so many wonderful places."

"How's it—"

A waitress came to take their orders. Mac prayed it wouldn't take long. Once she'd left, she tried again.

"How's it going with your doctor?"

"Really good."

Ivy looked beautiful—her red hair was lustrous, her face glowing, and her eyes radiant. She was in love. A pang of jealousy zapped Mac, and she closed her eyes.

"Are you all right, Mac?"

She smiled into Ivy's anxious eyes. "A touch of indigestion. Do you have any antacids or peppermints?"

"I think I have some breath mints." Ivy dug through her bag. "Here you go." She held the tin box out to Mac triumphantly.

"Thanks." Mac chewed the mints and pondered her next question. "I miss the good old days when you and I used to spend more time together."

"Me too." Ivy patted her hand. "Life gets busy."

"It does. I guess you don't have a lot of time now with work and David." Mac smiled at her. "What's he like?"

"He's wonderful."

"Where's he from?"

"Chicago, but he's lived all over. He did his residency in St. Louis. That's how he ended up here."

"Do you know where in St. Louis?"

"I think St. Louis University Medical School?" She scrunched up her mouth. "But I'm not sure."

"What's his specialty?"

"He's a cardiologist. A heart doctor." Ivy batted her eyelashes.

She had it bad. Mac prayed David Quinn wasn't in any way involved with Rosa or what happened to her.

The food arrived, and Mac let the conversation slip into how their families were and what they were doing for Thanksgiving. But part of her mind was stuck on Chicago. Rosa was from there.

"What's David doing for Thanksgiving?" Mac asked.

"I invited him over to my mom's house, but he already promised his aunt in St. Louis." Ivy stuck out her lip in a mock pouting gesture. "Maybe next year."

"I'm surprised a man who grew up in such a big city and

lived in large cities would like it here in Washington." Mac glanced at her friend to see what her reaction was.

"I know." Ivy nodded in agreement. "I asked him that very question the other day, and you know what he told me?"

"I can't imagine."

"Ivy, anyplace that has you in it has to be a great place." She put a hand over her heart. "Isn't that the sweetest thing you ever heard?"

"Yes, it is." Mac tightened her grip on her iced tea glass. And if the good doctor hurt her sweet, naïve friend, she would make him pay.

CHAPTER 24

On the porch outside the office, the familiar deep voice of Detective Jake Sanders sounded through the door. Mac's pulse quickened despite her resolve to focus on her work.

She pushed through the door, and the conversation stopped. Miss P, Sam, and Jake all looked at her as if she were some fragile thing about to break into a million pieces. She stomped across the floor.

Anger surged through her. If there was one thing she wasn't, it was delicate. She certainly didn't need their pity. "What?"

"Sit down." Jake pulled a chair out.

It was not a request. She sat. Anger fled, pushed out by a chill. What had happened?

"Rosa Lombardi had a heart attack."

"No, no, no." Mac jumped to her feet. "We visited her this morning."

Jake eased her down. "I know, but it's true. She's okay, but still in a coma."

"We need to find who shot her before it's too late." A hard fist of fear grew in her stomach.

"Yeah." He ran a hand through his hair. "I've instructed the hospital staff to keep quiet about her condition. Not to talk to anyone."

A dark premonition filled Mac's mind. "Whoever he is may try for Mr. Fischer. Especially if he thinks Fischer's helping Rosa make a new will."

"I've arranged for undercover security for Mr. Fischer, too."

"Okay. Let's get started." Mac rubbed her forehead and pulled a yellow pad in front of her. "We've got work to do."

"I'll go first if there are no objections." Miss P passed a sheet of paper to each of them. "Fischer Industries has hired four new employees in the last six months. Claudia Smith, Mr. Fischer's new assistant; the new maintenance man, Otis Miller; and two new research lab assistants. All their information is on the pages I handed out.

"What happened to Mr. Fischer's old assistant?" Jake asked.

"They offered her a job at Boeing in St. Louis that paid more with better benefits, and I'm told she always wanted to move to the big city."

"And the maintenance man?"

"They had one before, and he complained about needing help." Miss P adjusted her glasses. "The lab assistants were hired because the research department of Fischer Industries is growing. Both came with excellent references."

"There aren't any photos here," Sam said.

"Yes. I'm not sure what happened." Miss P peered at the print through her glasses. "I'll get them."

"Thanks, Miss P." Mac made notes on her handout and laid it aside.

"I'll do background checks on them and let you know." Jake

scribbled at the top of his page, folded the paper, and put it in his pocket.

"I guess I'll go next since mine is short and sweet," Sam said. "Nothing so far about Rosa's husband. I'll be glad to help with anything else."

"I've got something for you to research, Sam." Mac consulted her notes. "I had lunch with Ivy today, and she told me a little about Dr. David Quinn. She said he's from Chicago and did his residency at St. Louis Medical School. And he's supposed to have an aunt in St. Louis." Mac looked across the table at her friend and partner. "See what you can find on him."

"I will." Sam's fingers flew over her keyboard. "I may also see if I can find out what happened to Fischer's past assistant. It sounds fishy to me she would be offered a job at Boeing right at the same time Fischer Industries is bidding on one of their projects."

"Good catch. I didn't think of that," Mac said. "How's Alan?"

"He's getting better every day. Eager to get back to work."

"He doesn't really have to read through my old college newspapers."

"Don't tell him that. It makes him feel like he's doing something useful." Sam grinned. "At least for now."

"The only thing of interest would be past news of Nate I failed to see."

"Nothing so far."

Mac placed her pencil on her tablet. "Any suggestions where we go from here?"

"I need to get back to the precinct." Jake rose. "The Chief will want an update, and I want to get started on these background checks. I've added the good doctor to my list." He looked at Mac. "Walk me to my car?"

Her heart jumped into her throat. Again? "Sure."

At his patrol car, he placed a hand on her waist and drew her closer. "We need more time together. Just the two of us."

"Are you asking me on a date, Detective?"

"I guess I am." He gave her a lopsided grin.

She played with the collar on his shirt while her heart hammered in her chest. *Help me out here, Lord.* "When were you thinking about going on this date?"

"Sunday? We could eat at Marquarts and, if the weather's nice, walk along the river."

She caught her breath. Three days?

"Too soon?" he asked.

"No," she said—much to her surprise. "Sunday's fine."

A tiny feeling of unease rippled through her, and she couldn't help wondering not if—but what—would interrupt her second date with Detective Sanders.

Mac ignored the obvious questions in the looks she got from Sam and Miss P. "Right. Where were we?"

"We were trying to decide what direction to take next." Sam consulted her computer screen. "I think we—you and me —should pay a visit to Fischer Industries."

"I have a dear friend in the Records Department in Jefferson City who may help us with Rosa's marriage." Miss P made a notation on her calendar. "I'll call her and see about lunch."

"Great." Mac pushed her chair back. "I'll call Mr. Fischer and set up a time to go over there." She tapped her pencil against her pad. "We haven't investigated Rosa's family yet. We need to. When Sam and I speak to Mr. Fischer, we can ask him about them, but Miss P, would you be able to do some research as well?"

"Certainly." She peered at Mac over her glasses. "We believe the business to be based in Chicago?"

"Yes. We should have more after our visit with Mr. Fischer."

An edgy silence fell over the group. Mac dreaded her next words.

"Miss P—"

"Mackenzie—"

The two women gazed at each other.

"I know this is hard for you," Miss P said. "I loved my sister, but I hardly know my nephew or what Nathanial's been up to these past seven years. And I've never been one to either shy away from the truth or make excuses for unacceptable behavior."

"Thank you for understanding," Mac said. "I have a few questions. We'll talk later." Her phone rang. Jake. Unease prickled her skin.

"Rosa's had another heart attack."

CHAPTER 25

"We'll be right there." Mac bolted from her seat. "Come on, Sam. Rosa's had another heart attack."

Sam closed her computer and rushed into her office.

"If anyone calls, Miss P, don't tell them anything." Mac zipped her jacket and grabbed her purse. "Sam, come on."

"Of course." Miss P pressed her hands together. "I'll pray for her. And you. Be careful."

In the car, Mac growled at every red light and car that dared turn in front of them.

"What's your hurry?" Sam asked. "It will all be over by the time we get there."

"Don't say that." Mac shot her partner a scowl.

"I didn't mean she'd be dead." Sam lowered her voice. "Although you have to prepare yourself for the possibility, Mac."

She eased up on the accelerator. Sam was right, but the thought of Rosa dying before she talked to her left a hole. And she hated that feeling.

"Think positive." Sam took her arm as they crossed the

hospital parking lot. "Rosa's tough. She came through one heart attack."

But as soon as they got off the elevator, Mac knew. Jake stood outside Rosa's room, hands on hips and head down. Frustration, anger, and sorrow flooded through her, and she stumbled over to a chair set against the wall.

"You'll be okay." Sam sat beside her. "Remember who we are and why we're here. We can do something, Mac. We can find whoever did this to Rosa."

"You're the best friend and partner I could ever hope for." Mac reached for Sam's hand. "Thank you."

"Ditto." Sam rose. "Time to rock and roll, girlfriend."

As they approached Jake, he turned pain-filled eyes on Mac. "I'm sorry."

She nodded. "What now?"

"I've instructed the three nurses caring for her to keep this to themselves for as long as they can. Not to put it on her chart or alert the doctors. There shouldn't be anyone rounding on her since it's the weekend." He scrubbed a hand down his face. "We'll keep an officer outside the room as if nothing has happened, and the nurses will come and go as if doing whatever it is they do."

"Are we sure she had a heart attack, and it wasn't murder?"

"Yes, but right before the attack, her vitals spiked." Jake's brow furrowed. "I've asked my officer for a list of her visitors and the nurses for any recollection of what happened today."

"We're thinking someone may have gotten into her room and did what?" Sam asked.

"Put something in her IV?" Mac glanced at Jake and then Sam. "Or scared her to death?"

"The autopsy should show any elevated levels of a drug or a foreign substance," Jake said. "But scare her, how?"

"I don't know," Mac said. "But I have this gut feeling her

husband's here in Washington pretending to be someone else and orchestrating everything."

"So now we have to find her husband and his accomplice?"

"Yes."

"We're talking men new to the area."

"Yes, but he could have a female accomplice." A dull ache grew between her eyes. "When will they do the autopsy?"

"An ambulance will take the body to St. Louis County Morgue about midnight." Jake swiped his phone. "They've agreed to fast track it."

The body. *It.* Jake, the police officer, could distance himself from Rosa. Mac rubbed the bridge of her nose as tears pricked the backs of her eyes. Losing this woman felt like losing a part of herself. Which made no sense at all.

"Sam, you ready to go?" Mac zipped her coat. "I've got a headache."

"I'll walk out with you." Jake strode beside her.

As they stepped outside, Mac drew in the brisk air. Why did the cold air seem cleaner somehow? She let it out through her mouth in a puff of vapor.

"Are you all right?" Jake turned her to face him. "I know you felt a connection to Rosa."

She smiled. The cop was gone, and the kind man she cared about stood before her. "I'm fine. Thank you."

"I'm not sure what you're thanking me for, but I'll take it." He brushed a hand down her cheek. "I'll let you know about the autopsy as soon as I hear."

"Good." She nodded.

"Don't forget the background checks." Sam hugged her brother. "Now it's a murder investigation. We need to—"

"Rock and roll. I know."

Sam typed David Quinn's name into the attendance and degree verification database. Five entries came up. When she added the name of the university, it narrowed to two. One attended twenty-five years before the other. Father and son?

"Can you leave what you're doing?" Mac leaned into Sam's office, her hand on the doorknob. "Mr. Fischer said we could come over now."

"Let me finish this, and I'll be ready."

"I'll tell him we're on our way and meet you in the car."

Sam barely got her seatbelt clicked before Mac took off. "Hey. Slow down. We never talked about what we hope to learn from this meeting."

"Sorry." Mac threw her an apologetic look. "I want to know more about Rosa's family. And I'm still not convinced his fall was an accident."

"Remember, we agreed to help Mr. Fischer with his problem. I think we should start there. Then ask about new hires, get more details about the day he tripped, and end with details about Rosa." Sam checked her purse for a notebook and pen. "I'll take notes."

"You'll have to keep me on track."

Sam laughed to herself. So what else was new?

They parked as usual across the street from the buff-colored brick building. Mr. Fischer greeted them as they entered the foyer.

"Thanks for coming on short notice. This is a good time because Miss Smith is out on an errand."

Sam and Mac shared a quizzical look. Why was he so anxious to be rid of Miss Smith?

"I thought we would start with a brief survey of the labs and your office where the ... incidents have occurred," Mac said.

"My thoughts exactly. Follow me." Mr. Fischer led them to the back of the building.

Three high-ceilinged rooms opened into a hall. Their doors stood open, and the murmur of voices issued from each.

Mr. Fischer motioned to a man at a lab bench in the middle of the first room. "These ladies are private detectives I've hired to investigate the trouble we've been having. Please tell them what's happened here in the labs."

"Be glad to," the man said. "We thought we'd had notebooks with necessary data taken only to find them hidden a couple of days later—after we'd redone the experiments." He walked to a piece of equipment on a side bench. "He moved our balance to an office closet upstairs, and a portable scanner went missing for three days before we found it in a corner of the factory under a tarp. Those are a few examples of what has gone on here."

"Is there any pattern? Do they happen on the same day of the week? Or when the same people are in the labs?"

"I've tried to make sense of it, but no. And I can't believe anyone in the lab would do this. We're all at the breaking point with this jerk."

"Okay. Thanks." Mac strolled around the lab. "How would the guy know what to take?"

"Pardon me?"

"How would he know what stuff would mess up your experiments?"

"I ... don't know."

She ran a finger over the desktop. "Why weren't your notebooks locked in a drawer?"

"Nothing ever happened like this before. I guess we got complacent. Believe me, we make sure everything's locked up tight now."

"And yet Mr. Fischer told me something happened last week."

"I know." The man gave his head a brief shake, a puzzled look on his face. "I still can't figure that one out."

"What was it?" Sam asked.

"We found a file open on the bench when we came in. But it wasn't one of ours. It was old, and when we showed it to Mr. Fischer, he said it had been taken from his office."

"What was the file about?"

"The Lombardi Company." Mr. Fischer's quiet answer came from the doorway.

CHAPTER 26

S am saw Mac's eyes light up. If she didn't work fast, the agenda they'd agreed on for this meeting would go up in smoke.

"I think we have all we need here." She closed her notebook and gave Mac the Look. "Why don't we see your office next, Mr. Fischer?"

"Of course." He guided them down the hallway to an alcove that contained the elevator to the second floor. "I don't use the stairs these days."

"Good idea," Mac said.

They made the brief trip in silence and followed the owner of Fischer Industries the few steps to his office, where he eased into the big chair behind his desk.

"Please have a seat. There's water in the fridge if you would like. I'm going to ask you to get it yourself. Not very hospitable of me, but I'm sure you understand."

"Of course." Sam walked over to the small refrigerator.

After retrieving three waters, she took a seat in one of the comfortable armchairs in front of the desk. Wonder how much it would cost to get a couple of these for their office? She spied Mac running her hand over the leather and knew she was thinking the same thing.

Sam made a note at the top of the page to look into the chairs.

"Which drawers did you find open?" Maybe she could keep the topic on the Fischer problem for a while longer.

"The top middle and right lower."

"Do you keep keys in either drawer?"

"The lower right contains keys to my filing cabinet. I always thought they were safe because someone would have to open my desk first."

"Which is opened through your top middle drawer," Mac said.

"Yes." Mr. Fischer let out a long sigh. "None of my files have ever gone missing—until the one found in the lab downstairs."

"That you know of."

"After they found the Lombardi file, I did a thorough search. They're all there."

"I'd like to see—"

"Who has access to your office, Mr. Fischer?" Sam gave Mac a keep-with-the-program look, and Mac clamped her mouth shut.

"Miss Smith, my son—he's my COO—and the maintenance men. And I suppose the cleaners."

"You said you were glad we could come see you while Miss Smith was out. Why is that?" Mac asked.

"There's something about her." Fischer leaned on his desk. "I can't put my finger on it, but I'm not sure I trust her."

"But you hired her."

"She comes with excellent references, and she's very good at her job." He sighed. "Almost too good. She seems overqualified for the position."

"What about the maintenance man? Otis Miller?" Sam stopped writing. "What's your take on him?"

"He appears trustworthy." Fischer raised his eyebrows. "Why?"

"Did you believe him about the glue?"

"Oh yes. He seemed very sincere."

A pot of glue accidentally kicked over and left there for what? Hours? Until the president of the company happened to be coming down those very stairs.

A seed of an idea came to Sam. "Did you have any meetings the day you fell? Or visitors?"

"Let me check." He brought up his calendar on his computer. "No meetings. I ate lunch at my desk." He sat back in his chair. "I do recall two unexpected callers, though. Two new people to town."

Sam's heart beat faster, and she shared a glance with Mac.

"One was the new doctor in town. He wanted to let me know he was available if I wanted a doctor to come do routine checks on me or my employees. Nice young man. Dr. David Quinn, I believe." Fischer smiled. "The other was a new lawyer in town drumming up business. I told him I had a lawyer, but he insisted it didn't hurt to know the name of another one, just in case. I have his card." He opened his top drawer and drew out a business card. "Here it is."

Mac took it from his outstretched hand, and Sam bent to read the name she knew would be there. Nathanial Xander Westcott III.

"In fact, I decided to work with him on drawing up Rosa's will. We're meeting tomorrow to finalize it."

Mac had a coughing spasm. Sam handed her an open bottle of water.

"It's okay," Sam whispered. "Take a deep breath."

"What is it?" Worry darkened every crease on Mr. Fischer's face. "Miss Love, are you okay?"

"She's fine." Sam gave a reassuring smile. "She's very concerned about Rosa. Especially since Mac's kidnapping. And then Rosa's shooting."

"Yes. Poor girl. I wish I could see her."

"I know, but she's in a coma and under guard. Only her doctors and nurses are let in to see her."

"And her lawyer, Mr. Westcott," Mr. Fischer said. "He told me he could see her because he works as a lawyer for her family. That's why I decided to use him to help draw up her will."

Sam clutched the arm of the chair. Had she heard correctly? Had Nate been in Rosa's hospital room?

"Do you know when he visited her?" Sam heard the shake in her voice but couldn't control it.

Fischer stiffened. "I'm not sure. Does it matter?"

"No." Mac said. "It surprised us. Nate is Miss P's nephew, and we've gotten to know him. He's aware we're working on her case, but he's never mentioned being the family lawyer to her or to us."

"I'm sure that has to do with lawyer/client privilege, don't you?"

"Yes."

"Mr. Fischer, we won't take up any more of your time, but one last thing. Could we borrow the Lombardi file you have?"

"Here you are. Take it with you. But please, return it when you're through." He started to rise from his chair.

"No. Don't get up. We can see ourselves out." Sam stood, and Mac followed. "Thanks for all your time. We'll call you if we think of any more questions or if we find an answer to what's been happening here."

"I look forward to hearing from you. I have faith in you two."

Sam hustled Mac out the door and across the street to the car. They sat in stunned silence for a few moments.

"I guess we know now why Nate hasn't been around the office." Sam looked at Mac, her beautiful face distorted with anger. "Remember, partner, there are always two sides to every story."

"Hmm. I can't wait to hear what Nathanial Xander Westcott III has to say for himself," Mac said through gritted teeth.

Neither could Sam. She started the car and backed out.

"Two new professional men come to Washington in the last six months," Sam said. "Both visited Mr. Fischer on the day he fell down the stairs. One visited Rosa in the hospital—and maybe the other as well. I'll check when we get back to the office."

"One of them came to kill Rosa." Mac's words echoed in Sam's heart and soul. But which one?

CHAPTER 27

Ten minutes later, they pulled into the driveway of their office. Mac caught Sam's arm before she got out of the car. "It's late, and I'm tired. Let's go home and pick up again in the morning."

"My family will appreciate it. See you tomorrow."

As Mac negotiated the familiar streets leading to her house, her mind chased down question after question. She hit the garage door button. As she pulled in and exited the car, two men in black ducked in after her.

"What—"

They each grabbed one of her arms. Mac threw herself from side to side, hoping to break their hold.

"We will not hurt you," one of them yelled.

"I'm tired of being attacked and kidnapped." Anger and frustration gushed through her and out of her mouth. "I'm not Rosa."

"We know."

"Then why?" she screamed.

"The boss needs you." They slapped duct tape on her mouth and dragged her toward their car parked on the street.

Mac went limp. Her sudden dead weight pulled the men down. She launched her head at the face of the man on her right. A crunch, and he loosened his grip.

She pivoted and drove her knee into the other man's groin. Yanking her arms free, she cringed as he bent double.

A pair of headlights swung around the corner. The thugs hobbled to their car. As they screeched away from the curb, she ripped the tape from her mouth.

Jake stopped in front of her house and jumped out. "What's going on?"

"They tried to kidnap me again." She ran for Jake's police car. "Come on. We can catch them if we hurry."

"Are you hurt?"

"No," she growled, still too angry to accept his kindness. "They're getting away."

Jake took off in the direction of the dark sedan. At the cross street, he slowed. No taillights anywhere. The streets were empty.

"We lost them." Mac cracked her window and listened for engine sounds. "It's too dark to search for them. Might as well go back."

At her house, Mac made a pot of coffee. "Thank God you pulled up when you did." She handed Jake a mug. "Or I might be on a private jet to Chicago by now."

"Seemed to me like you didn't need any help. Did they say why?"

She shook her head. "Only that the boss needed me. For what, I can't imagine, and I'm too tired to even try."

"I came over to give you Rosa's preliminary autopsy report." Jake took a drink and sat back in his chair. "I almost called, but for some reason, I felt the need to come in person. I'm glad I did, or I might have missed the show."

"Hah, hah." Mac pulled her legs under her on the couch. "What have they found out?"

"No sign of elevated drugs or any foreign substance in her blood."

"That rules out anything put into her IV."

Jake nodded. "And the pathologist said her adrenaline levels were high, but those aren't a reliable indicator of being scared to death. They vary too much from person to person."

"But it's a possibility?"

"A very slight one. They still have more to do. We'll get a full autopsy report tomorrow or the next day."

"But someone did shoot her."

"Yep." Jake peered at Mac over the rim of his mug. "Technically, she died from complications due to wounds inflicted by an unknown gunman."

"Yes." Mac unfolded her legs and stood. "More coffee? I need to tell you about our talk with Mr. Fischer today."

Jake listened to her story without interruption. She liked that in him. When she talked to him, he paid attention. At the end, she asked for his thoughts.

"It's a lot to digest all at one time. All the potential connections." He studied his hands. "Have Sam send me a copy of her notes. I'll show them to the Chief. At some point, we'll need to sit down together and hash this out."

Another thing Mac liked about Jake. He didn't rush into conclusions—like she did sometimes. He raised his eyes to hers, and his gaze took her breath away.

"I'm arranging for a car outside your house until we either figure out what's going on here or catch the goons who tried to snatch you tonight." Jake pushed to his feet. He picked up his mug.

"I'll take care of your cup." Mac reached for it.

He wrapped an arm around her and drew her close. Before she could move away, he pressed his lips to hers, and she kissed him back. One serious kiss that left her wanting more. He released her and headed for the door.

"See you tomorrow." He winked at her as he pulled the door shut behind him.

Mac watched through the sheers on her front window as a squad car pulled up across the street, and Jake trotted over to the driver's side. After a moment, he got in his own car and drove off.

In the kitchen, she put the mugs in the dishwasher, cleaned the coffeepot, and set it up for the morning brew. Her phone chimed. An unknown number. Should she answer? She pressed the green button and held it to her ear.

"Miss Love?" A mechanical voice spoke in her ear. "Are you there? This is Rosa's father."

Silence. Every nerve in Mac's body came alive.

"I don't blame you for not wanting to speak to me. Please listen. I have a proposition for you. I know my baby girl is in a hospital in a coma, but I am in trouble. I need her here to vote on something of great importance for the future of our company. That is where you come in."

Pause.

"I need your help."

Mac couldn't stand it any longer. "And you thought the way to get me to help you was to send your goons to kidnap me?"

"I am sorry. That was a mistake. I should have contacted you as I am doing now."

"What is it you want from me?" She paced around her house.

"As we both know, you could be my Rosa's twin. I am

asking you to come to Chicago and stand in for her. We would dress you like Rosa, fix your hair like she does, and all you would have to do is sit in the meeting and vote the same way I do. A mere nod of the head or slight raise of the hand. That's all required."

"You're telling me no one will realize I'm not Rosa?" Mac stopped in front of a mirror.

"No. She has spent little time here. We are not close."

"How do I know Rosa would vote the way you want me to?"

"In this case, I can assure you she would. And so would you."

"Let me think about it."

"The meeting is Monday evening. I will call again on Sunday."

The line went dead. A whisper of unease ran through her. What would happen to her when she said no?

CHAPTER 28

The headlights of Jake's police issue SUV swept across the dark front of his house as he turned into his driveway. He snatched the takeout bag from Cowan's Restaurant from his front seat and swung his legs out of the vehicle.

As he stepped inside, he shook the bag. "Duchess. I've got chicken from Cowan's."

"Mwrwr." Like a gray ghost, his cat appeared, her emerald green eyes shining up at him.

"Thought you might like something different for dinner." Jake stooped to put chicken pieces in her dish before retrieving a hamburger and fries for himself.

He grabbed a soda from the fridge and sat at the table. How many meals had he eaten like this? Alone except for his cat. Too many. He wanted what Sam had with Alan. He wanted Mac.

But every time he decided he couldn't live without her, thoughts of his dad's illness, and the pain his mom was going through took a hatchet to his dreams. Was it worth it? His eyes wandered to where his phone lay on the table. He knew who he needed to talk to.

"Mom? Got a minute?"

"Jake? Are you okay?"

He'd scared her.

"I'm fine. I just want to talk to you about ..." About what? Dad? Love? Life? All three? "I don't know."

"Why don't you come get me, and we'll go for coffee," she said in a soft voice.

"Yeah. Good idea." His spirits lifted. She always knew what he needed.

Duchess rubbed against his leg and purred. He picked her up.

"Don't be too late tonight. I'll be gone for a couple of hours."

The sleek gray cat pressed her head against his chin and leaped to the floor.

Jake shook his head in wonder. Sometimes he thought she actually understood him.

AFTER HER STRANGE PHONE CALL, Mac had found it hard to sleep and debated calling Jake. But what good would that do? She'd see him today—if she could keep her eyes open. She yawned and hunched over her mug. Maybe the steam would help the bags under her eyes.

Her phone's piercing ring sounded, and she picked it up.

"Hello, Mr. Fischer." She stifled another yawn. "What can I do for you?"

"We need to meet at your office. I have something you will want to see."

"What is it?"

"I received a registered letter from Rosa Lombardi."

"I can be at the office in fifteen minutes." Mac sat her mug on the counter. "And, Mr. Fischer, do not tell anyone else about this."

"Hmm. I'm afraid that may be a problem."

"Why?"

"Dr. Quinn was with me when it was delivered. He performed a wellness check on me after my hospital stay." Fischer paused. "And I called Mr. Westcott to cancel our meeting today."

"You didn't tell him why, did you?"

"I'm afraid I did."

Mac groaned. "Okay. Listen, change of plans. Stay at your office. Lock your door and don't let anyone in until I get there with Detective Sanders."

"Mackenzie, what is going on?"

"I'll explain when I get there."

She raced to her bedroom, her phone to her ear. "Pick up Jake," she muttered to herself.

"Good morning, Mac."

His deep voice brought back his kiss from the night before and, for an instant, she forgot why she called.

"Meet me at Fischer Industries. Right away." She grabbed a sweater and jeans from her closet. "Mr. Fischer got a letter from Rosa, and he's holed up in his office waiting for us to arrive."

"Rosa?"

"Yes. She must have mailed it before she got here." Mac pulled on socks and boots. "She wasn't coming to Mr. Fischer for help with her will. She was coming to make sure he'd implement it if anything happened to her."

"Be there in ten."

Another thing she liked about Jake. When it was time to

act, he didn't hesitate. She slung her purse over her shoulder and hurried to her car. On the way, she called Sam at the office.

"I'll meet you at the factory."

Mac arrived at Fischer Industries to find Jake and Samantha waiting for her outside the front door. A strange, cold excitement filled her whole being as they entered the building and climbed the staircase to the second floor.

When they entered the outer office, Claudia Smith stood.

"He's expecting us." Mac marched over to Fischer's office door and knocked. "Mr. Fischer, it's me, Mackenzie Love, and Detective Sanders."

Fischer unlocked the door and allowed them inside. "Miss Smith, please see that I'm not disturbed." He locked the door behind them.

A manila envelope lay on the conference table in the middle of the room. Mac, Sam, and Jake pulled gloves on and walked toward it.

"Have you opened it?" Mac asked.

"The manila envelope, yes, but not the two inside. I thought it best to have witnesses."

"Good thinking." Mac looked at Jake and Sam. "How should we go about this?"

"Since it's addressed to Mr. Fischer, he should open it." Jake handed him a pair of gloves. "Who's handled the letter so far?"

"Someone in the mailroom, Miss Smith, and me."

Jake nodded. "We'll get fingerprints later."

Mr. Fischer extracted two white letter-sized envelopes from the larger manila envelope. The thin one had Mr. Fischer's name on it. The thick one bore the label of The Legal Will and Testament of Rosa Marie Lombardi.

"Now you see why I felt the need to cancel my appointment with Mr. Westcott."

"I do." Mac touched the bulging envelope where it lay on the table. "I only wish you hadn't told him why."

"I don't understand." Mr. Fischer slumped into a chair. "What did I do wrong?"

"You did nothing wrong. On purpose." Sam's delicate face clouded with sadness. "But we have some things to share with you."

Sam was right. Mr. Fischer needed to know the truth. Mac took a seat across from him and motioned for Sam and Jake to sit as well.

"Mr. Fischer, Rosa is dead. She died from a heart attack yesterday."

"Oh, no." He leaned an elbow on the table and put his head in his hand. "Poor girl."

He stared at Mac, and she read the question there.

"We couldn't tell you sooner because we believe her husband is here in Washington and working with an accomplice to kill her." She leaned forward. "We needed you to continue to draw up a will for her as if she was alive. Her killers are smart. They may have been able to figure it out if you were only going through the motions."

"*Did* they kill her?"

"Yes," Mac said. "And no. She died from complications from her gunshot."

Jake folded his hands in his lap. "But we're waiting on the final autopsy to say for sure."

"Who do you suspect?"

Mac cast a look at Sam and Jake before answering. "We're looking at Dr. Quinn and Nathanial Westcott."

Fischer paled. "I can see why you got so upset when I told you I called Westcott. Hopefully, this letter holds a clue." Mr. Fischer lifted the envelope addressed to him and slit it open.

He read the single sheet of paper before he passed it across the table to Mackenzie.

A range of emotions played across his face, from a tender smile to the tightness of stony anger to a dark-eyed sadness. Mac dropped her gaze to the letter before her.

Dear Mr. Fischer,

My mother always thought so highly of you and your wife, Jean. Her trips to visit you and your family in Washington were the highlight of her year. I was too young to remember details from those visits, but the memories I have are happy ones. Thank you for those and for being such good friends to my mother.

In the past years, things have been rough. I don't get along with my father. He tricked my mother into allowing certain foreign investors into the company, who pressured him into lowering his standards. After Mother's death, I've worked hard to counteract their influence with no success.

And I've made a terrible mistake of my own. I married a man I thought I loved and who loved me. Mother told me you know our history, so you're aware that she left the majority shares to me.

But the entire story is too long and complicated to tell in this letter. Let me say the sins of the parents do fall on the children, and I'm afraid for my life. My enemy wants a controlling interest in the company, and that will not happen if I can help it. I've drawn up a will, and I pray you will execute it for me.

It's all very legal, and all I ask of you is to hold on to it until you receive notice of my death. Then make sure it gets to the authorities.

My mother trusted you, Mr. Fischer, and so do I. Thank you from the bottom of my heart.

I'll try to come see you to make sure you received this before I disappear for good.

Sincerely,
Rosa Lombardi

CHAPTER 29

Mac passed the piece of paper to Jake and Sam. The letter hadn't told them anything they didn't already know. She still didn't know the name of Rosa's husband. Or what he looked like. But something about the letter nagged at her. What did she mean about the sins of the parents?

"The sins of the parents?" Jake asked.

"I believe she's referring to her mother's marriage to her father, a man who was only interested in her money, and now she, too, had fallen into the same trap." Sadness flickered in Mr. Fischer's eyes. "Except her situation proved fatal."

"What foreign interests is she's talking about." Sam handed Rosa's letter back to Mr. Fischer.

"It could be anyone." Fischer removed his reading glasses.

"I wonder if that's what the important vote is about on Monday," Mac said.

"What important vote?"

She hadn't told them.

"Don't get mad." She held up a hand. "I got the call late last night, but I was distracted by Mr. Fischer and his registered mail, and I just now remembered."

"What phone call?" Jake asked.

"It was after you left last night." Mac folded her hands on the table. "An unknown caller with a device that makes your voice sound like a robot."

"Great." Jake rubbed his forehead. "What did the robot say?"

"He said he was Rosa's father."

Sam's eyes grew wide, and Jake drew his hands into fists as she told them about her late-night call.

"Why didn't you call me right away?" Jake growled.

"What could you have done?" Mac stared him down. "I intended to tell you first thing this morning, but then I got the call from Mr. Fischer."

"Okay." Jake closed his eyes for a moment. "I get it."

A secretive smile softened her lips. Apology accepted.

"But we'll be ready when he calls again on Sunday." Jake leaned back and crossed his arms over his chest.

"Yes, sir."

Sam grabbed Mac's arm before she could salute.

Jake narrowed his eyes at Mac before he turned his attention to Mr. Fischer. "We need to get Rosa's will to a safe place."

"I have a safe here in my office." Fischer rose and walked behind his desk.

"No offense, sir, but in view of the problems you've been having, I suggest we find a different location."

"Yes, I see what you mean." The older man sat in his desk chair. "Where do you suggest?"

"You mentioned a lawyer you've used for years?"

"Yes. Unfortunately, his office is closed today," Mr. Fischer said. "Too many out with the flu."

"We have a safe at our offices." Sam looked to Mac for agreement. "We could keep it there until your lawyer gets back."

Mac nodded.

"Should we read it first?"

All eyes were on the fat white envelope on the conference table. The police officer in Jake pushed for keeping it confidential until they could get to a lawyer, but his gut screamed they should not only read it but copy it. Just in case.

"Since none of us stands to inherit anything, we should make a copy of it, and the letter." Jake squared his shoulders, ready for any opposition.

"I agree," Sam said.

"Me too." Mac nodded her head.

Mr. Fischer returned to the table and took the envelope in his hands.

Loud voices sounded from outside Mr. Fischer's door. The knob shook, followed by pounding.

"Mr. Fischer. It's urgent I speak with you." Nate's voice resonated through the solid oak door.

"Put the documents in your desk." Jake drew his pistol and held it by his side. He motioned Mac and Sam behind him. "Let him in. Let's see what he has to say."

Fischer unlocked the door.

"I'm sorry, sir," Miss Smith said. "I tried to tell him you were not to be disturbed."

"It's fine." Mr. Fischer stepped back as Nate barreled through the door.

He pulled up short when he saw Jake, Mac, and Sam there as well.

"I ..." Nate began to speak and stopped.

"Do you have any weapons on you?"

"No." The pitch of Nate's voice rose an octave.

Jake holstered his pistol, stepped over to Nate, and frisked him. "What's so urgent it couldn't wait?"

"I need to see Rosa Lombardi's will." Nate blinked. "To authenticate it."

"And how could you do that?" Mac asked. "I wasn't aware you knew her."

"I couldn't tell you, Mac." He moved in her direction, eyes soft and pleading.

"So, the whole time I was mistaken for Rosa, you knew what was happening." Color spread across Mac's neck and face.

If Jake didn't step in, things could get ugly. "Mac, we've got more important things to think about right now." He used his most authoritative tone—and it worked.

She glanced at him and retreated behind Mr. Fischer's desk.

"I'm afraid you've made the trip here for nothing, Mr. Westcott." Mr. Fischer took Nate by the arm and steered him to the door. "I intend to turn Miss Lombardi's will over to our family lawyers for execution."

"But what if it's a fake?"

"I'm sure they're smart enough to determine an improper will." Fischer opened the door and gave Nate a push into the outer office. "Miss Smith will see you out."

"Good job, Mr. Fischer." Jake slapped him on the back. "Now, where were we?"

"We were about to make a copy of the will and the letter." Mac withdrew the envelopes from Fischer's desk. "Where's your machine?"

"Another problem," Mr. Fischer said. "Miss Smith makes all my copies."

"We can do it at our offices." Mac stuffed the envelopes into her handbag. "We'll meet you there."

"I'll walk Mr. Fischer to his car. Then come back for you two." Jake shrugged his jacket on over his shoulders.

"You don't need to walk us out." Mac zipped her coat. "We can drive to the offices on our own."

Jake counted to three. "You've got the documents."

"But nobody knows that." She smiled sweetly at him.

Arguing with her was futile. He escorted Mr. Fischer out the door. On the way through the outer office, the CEO stopped at his assistant's desk.

"Miss Smith, I'm going out for a while. I'll be back later after the meeting with the City Council at four-thirty."

"Yes, sir," Claudia Smith said. "Is there anything I can do while you're out?"

"See if there's anyone at my lawyer's firm who can make me an appointment with him at his earliest convenience."

"Yes, sir."

As they entered the small elevator, Mr. Fischer leaned against the rail. "I met Rosa's mother in college."

"I wondered how you knew her," Jake said.

"She was amazing. One of very few women who attended a university in those days. Not to mention going for an engineering degree."

"Rosa's mother was an engineer?" Jake couldn't hide his astonishment.

"Almost. She didn't finish. She met Rosa's father and fell in love." Fischer's mouth spread into a grim line. "A waste of a good mind. Still, she knew enough to help run the company. If he'd listened to her."

"Why didn't he?"

"Like many men, he thought he knew best. He felt the need to control everything. Even his wife. He lost her in the end."

The elevator chugged its way to a stop on the first floor, and the doors opened. Something Fischer said pinched Jake's conscience like an ill-fitting shoe. But he'd have to think about that later.

At the front door, Jake motioned Fischer to wait until he could look outside. All clear. The two men walked along the sidewalk, Jake with his hand on Fischer's back until they got to the corner of the building.

"Which car is yours?" Jake asked.

"The dark blue Mercedes." Fischer angled across the parking lot toward his vehicle.

"Click it open."

A boom ruptured the quiet of midday.

CHAPTER 30

Car sirens screamed. Orange flames and billowing black smoke filled the sky. Metal wreckage strewn across the gravel parking lot, the sidewalk, and the street. The blood pounding in Mac's ears muffled the roaring fire, and the only things she had eyes for were two still figures surrounded by debris.

She pushed aside a man in uniform overalls kneeling next to Jake and pressed her fingers to his neck. The strong beat of his heart pushed back. *Thank you, Jesus.*

"Is he ...?" Sam dropped beside her.

"He's alive." Mac moved to Mr. Fischer and repeated her actions. "Mr. Fischer too."

"We've called 911." Claudia Smith stood over them, her eyes darting between the two prone figures and the crowd gathered nearby.

Mac scanned the people surrounding them. What was Smith looking for?

The familiar wails of emergency vehicles approaching caused a stir in the small throng of onlookers. A firetruck pulled into the parking lot followed by an ambulance. Jake moaned and lifted his arm.

"How's Fischer?"

"He's unconscious, but alive." Mac eased his arm down by his side. "Don't move until the paramedics check you over."

"I'm fine."

"I know, but do this for me."

"Okay." His voice was barely above a whisper.

"Where am I?" Mr. Fischer struggled to sit up.

Sam crawled over and convinced him to stay still. Mac shared a look of relief with her over the two men. Praise God, they were both alive.

Efficient as always, the EMTs had both men loaded into ambulances and headed for the hospital in a matter of minutes.

"I'll put these in our safe and meet you at the hospital." Mac checked her purse for the documents. Still there. "Go. You need to get your mom."

"Thanks, Mac." Sam squeezed her arm and jogged across the street toward her car.

"Miss Love, is there anything I can do?" Claudia Smith asked.

Mac eyed her. "Not right now, but I would like to talk to you later."

"Yes, I imagined you would." A calm smile lifted the corners of her mouth. "I think it's time."

Mac studied her retreating frame. Claudia Smith was a very cool and composed lady. Before Mr. Fischer's assistant entered the building, she scrutinized her surroundings once more. Her behavior put Mac on high alert. Maybe she needed to rethink her own safety precautions.

She readjusted her purse and re-zipped her jacket. She could put her collapsible baton in her pocket. Or a pocketknife.

Or both. With her luck, her pants would fall from the weight, and she'd trip.

At the car, Mac threw her purse on the seat next to her and backed out. She turned left onto Pine Street. The only stop sign between Fischer Industries and their offices was at the corner of Pine and Second.

She stopped, turned on her blinker, and prepared to go. A car screeched to a halt in front of her. Another bumped her from behind. Two men in black jumped out and one smashed in her passenger side window with a metal bar. He reached in and grabbed her purse.

Anger spiraled from the pit of her stomach. In one fluid move, she unsnapped her belt and seized her purse before it disappeared out the window.

"No." She roared and yanked with all her might. The strap broke, and Mac fell back against her door. The contents of her purse spilled onto the passenger seat on top of the shattered glass—including two white envelopes. She lunged for them, but the man was quicker.

"I've got them. Let's get out of here." He ran for his vehicle.

She scrambled for her phone among the items from her purse, jumped out of her car, and took photos as fast as she could of the retreating cars. "I hope one of these will be good."

Two nondescript white sedans would be hard to find unless she caught part of a license plate or some other distinguishing feature. They had on black balaclavas, so she didn't hold out any hope for a face. Unless—one of them took it off as he drove away?

Mac touched her cross. *Lord, I could use Your help—again.*

An unmarked SUV pulled up behind her. and Detective Victor Young climbed out. "We've got to stop meeting like this."

Mac forced a chuckle.

He spied her passenger window. "What happened there?"

"I'll tell you in a minute. Have you heard anything about Jake and Mr. Fischer?"

"Yes. Both are good."

"Thank You, God." Tension bled from Mac's spine, and she let her shoulders drop. "They ambushed me, leaving Fischer Industries."

"Who are you talking about? And what were they after?"

"I didn't get a good look at them. They were after something they thought they got. That's why they left." Mac grinned. "But I outsmarted them." She pulled the letter and Rosa's will from inside her jacket. "Follow me to my office. I've got to put these documents in the safe."

"Should I call forensics to fingerprint your car?"

"No. They both wore gloves." Mac shot a sour look at the mess next to her. "I just got this car."

"Don't worry. It won't be hard to fix. Soon it'll be good as new." Vic stepped back. "Let's go. I'll be right behind you."

Mac turned right onto Second and drove the four blocks to her office. As she exited her car, Miss P met her on the porch, a hand on her chest.

"I heard about the car exploding at Fischer Industries. Was anyone hurt?"

"The blast knocked Jake and Mr. Fischer to the ground, but they'll be okay." Mac gave her arm a reassuring squeeze. "I need to get into the safe, but first I want you to make copies of both these documents."

"I'll be right back."

"What will you do with the copies?" Detective Young asked.

"I'm not sure. We should have a second secure location for them."

"I have a safe at my home, Mackenzie. I will be glad to put

them there if you wish." Miss P handed her the originals and the copies.

"Thanks, Miss P, but I don't think that's a good idea." Mac looked at her feet. How could she tell her old friend her nephew was a suspect?

"Of course. I wasn't thinking." Miss P waved a dismissive hand in the air. "Nathanial is a suspect, I'm sure, and he's staying with me. If anything happened to the papers, I would be a suspect as well."

Max drew in a breath and let it out. "Yes. Sorry."

"What about your safe deposit box at the bank?"

"Good idea. I'll put the originals in the safe here, and if I hurry, I can get the copies to my bank before they close."

Only Mac and Sam knew where the safe was and the combination, and that's the way they wanted to keep it.

She paused by her desk and opened the top right drawer. It was time to carry a gun. The revolver was too heavy. Instead, she hefted her Sig in her hand before stuffing it into her purse. One last thing. She went to her closet.

"I'm ready to go, Vic."

"I'll drive. We can visit Jake and Mr. Fischer after you're done."

"Your poor purse." Miss P ran a finger gently over the worn leather.

"It'll do. I tied the strap ends together for now until I can get a replacement." Mac laughed. "I feel like this poor purse about now. Two frayed ends tied in knots."

"Which bank?" Vic led her out to his police vehicle. The sun was down, and shadows deepened all around them.

"Bank of Washington on Main."

He turned on his headlights, backed out of the driveway, and headed east into town. "By the way, what was in the envelopes the guy stole from your car?"

"The fat one contained a brochure from the dealer where I bought my car." Mac snorted. "And the other one had a blank piece of paper in it."

"How did you—"

A pickup slammed into the left front fender. The SUV slid to the right.

Mac stifled a scream. She jammed her hand into her purse and removed her pistol.

"Stay calm." Vic spoke into his police radio. "Accident at Second and Pine. Officer involved."

Two men jumped from the truck.

"Get in back and take cover." Vic unsnapped his holster and withdrew his gun.

"I can help," she said, her mind and body on high alert.

"Just do it." His words hit her across the face like a whip.

She threw her purse over the seat and dove after it. But she kept a tight grip on her pistol.

He threw his door open and sprang to the pavement. "Police. You're under—"

Her heart leaped into her throat as a burst of gunfire overpowered Vic's words.

"I'm hit." A voice she didn't recognize.

Mac raised her head above the seat enough to see two shadows at the truck. One bent over the other. She looked down. Vic's leg was visible through his door. It wasn't moving.

"Get the girl."

The girl. Every nerve sparked and shuddered. She flung her door open and bounded from the SUV, vaguely aware of the weight of the gun in her hand.

Footsteps pounded after her.

She ran into the welcoming cover of darkness of a clump of trees. The footsteps slowed. Pressed against the largest pine, she hazarded a glance. Her pursuer stood fifteen feet away, listening intently.

"I know you're in there, Miss Love." He peered into the small clump of trees where she hid. "That was a clever trick you played on us before. But did you think we'd give up that easy?" He raised his gun and shot into the darkness a few feet away from her head.

Her mind played tricks on her, and she was back in the operating room at the hospital with a knife at her throat. Adrenaline surged through her. She stepped from behind the tree, raised the gun in her hand, and fired.

The blow to her chest knocked her backwards against an oak. Her knees buckled, and she slid to the ground, gasping for breath.

CHAPTER 31

Mac clutched the pillow as she lay in the emergency room. The nightmare played out over and over in her mind. In slow motion, the bullet left her gun, and the man fell to the ground. But not before he shot her. Her stomach clenched, and she groaned.

Miss P patted her arm. "Praise God, you put on your armored vest, Mackenzie."

Chief Baker stormed into the room. "Miss Love, how many more of my men have to end up in the hospital before you solve your case?"

"Thomas Baker, Miss Love is in no shape for any of your bullying." The man's former chemistry teacher stepped between the Chief of Police and her friend. "Besides, it's not her fault the criminal element in this town is alive and well." She peered at him over her glasses.

Mac cringed and waited for the explosion. None came.

"Miss Freebody, I apologize." The Chief removed his hat. "My concern for my men got the better of me. I will need a statement from Miss Love as soon as possible."

"I promise, Chief." Mac closed her eyes.

"I will accompany her," Miss P said.

A nurse came into the room and looked at the Chief. "Are you here about Detective Young?"

The Chief nodded.

"He's out of surgery and listed as critical. He's got a long recovery ahead of him. They recovered the bullet. You'll have to see the surgeon to retrieve it."

"When can I see Vic?"

"He's in ICU. Only family allowed now." The nurse glanced between Mac and the Chief. "You'll have to arrange a time to get his statement when the doctor feels he's strong enough."

The Chief furrowed his brow. Mac knew that wasn't what he wanted to hear.

"What about Detective Sanders?" she asked. "And Mr. Fischer?"

"They're being held overnight. Both should be able to go home tomorrow."

"And the other man?" Mac held her breath.

The nurse lowered her clipboard. "He almost didn't make it. If the ambulance hadn't shown up when it did, he would have bled out."

"I aimed for his leg, but it was dark."

"You hit his leg, but you nicked the femoral artery."

Mac hugged her pillow tighter and moaned. *Thank You, Jesus.*

Chief Baker sat next to her bed. "First time you shot anyone, huh?"

She nodded.

"My first time, I got sick. It wasn't pretty." He sighed. "I'm sorry you had to fire your gun, but you did the right thing. You did good."

Mac took in the Chief's serious profile. He wasn't one to

share or offer words of sympathy. She'd hug him, but she wasn't one to hug—even if she'd been in any shape to do so.

"Thanks, Chief."

"You're welcome. Don't tell anybody about the sick thing."

"I won't."

"I need to see Sanders. You want to come?" The Chief pushed to his feet.

"Yes." Mac searched for Miss P. "Can you see if I can get out of here?"

"Certainly."

Miss P returned with a wheelchair. "You can go see your friends provided you travel in this."

On the elevator, it was only the three of them. The Chief turned to Mac. "Why are those men coming after you?"

"They want Rosa Lombardi's will. I've got a copy in my purse. The original is in my safe at the office."

"They're willing to kill my officer and you for a copy?"

The elevator stopped, and the doors opened. After making sure no one was within earshot, Mac continued their conversation. "They must think it's the original. I was trying to get to my bank to put it in my safe deposit box when they attacked me."

"Have you read it?"

"No. We agreed to wait until we could get it to Mr. Fischer's lawyer."

Chief Baker held the door for Mac and Miss P. Jake lay in the bed surrounded by Sam, Alan, and his mother. Happiness sprang up in Mac's heart at the sight of her friends. Sam's beautiful smile welcomed them in, and Alan went in search of more chairs.

"I won't be staying." Chief Baker removed his hat and smoothed his balding head. "I wanted to make sure you were in good hands." He pursed his lips. "Don't get soft on me, Sanders."

"I won't, sir. If the doctor didn't insist on one more night, I'd be back today."

"Tomorrow's fine. Bright and early." He stuck his hat on and gave a slight bow to the ladies. "Glad you're okay, son."

Alan wrestled two chairs through the door. He scanned the room. "Where'd the Chief go?"

"He couldn't stay. While we're all together, why don't we compare notes?" She shifted in her wheelchair. "I don't know how much longer I can stand to sit in this thing."

"Notes about what?" Sam asked.

Mac took a deep breath. "Since you came to the hospital, and I left with Rosa's will, I've been attacked twice. Detective Young was shot and is in the ICU, and I shot one of my attackers."

"And they shot you too." Miss P folded her hands in her lap.

A heavy silence descended on the room, followed by a storm of voices.

Mac held up her hands. "All your questions will get answered if you'll let me tell you what happened."

As she related the incidents of the past few hours, each of her friends listened without saying a word. Sam took notes.

When she finished, Gloria Sanders raised her hand.

"Mom, you don't have to hold up your hand to speak in this group." Sam smiled at her.

"I was thinking we should pray for Detective Young—and the poor misguided man who attacked you. And of course, for Mackenzie."

"Yes, we should," Miss P stood and held her hands out. Everyone followed and joined hands. "Mrs. Sanders, perhaps you would lead us in prayer."

Mac caught Sam's eye. She remembered holding hands and praying with Mr. Fischer in the hospital not long ago.

When they had finished and returned to their seats, Mac consulted the notes on her phone. "Do we know yet if Dr. Quinn was one of Rosa's doctors?"

"Yes." Sam thumbed through her pages. "He checked on her the morning she died."

"Who else was in her room that day?" Mac's pulse picked up.

"From the officer on duty, it seems Nate popped in for a second, a cleaner, and the nurses, of course."

"Why would Nate be there?"

"What has my nephew got himself into?" Miss P pressed her hand to her chest.

"I think it's time to get Nathanial Xander Westcott III in for a little chat." Jake pushed himself up in his bed. "If they'll ever let me out of here."

CHAPTER 32

Two chief suspects. Both professional men. Both would be easy to check on. And yet, Mac experienced a strong sense she'd missed something. She read through her notes.

"Have we checked alibis for the night someone shot Rosa?"

"The police did," Sam said. "Doctor Quinn was with Ivy the first part of the night, but their date ended in plenty of time for him to get over to the camp. He says he went straight home to bed, but nobody can vouch for him."

"What about Nathanial?" Miss P asked.

"I can answer part of that," Mac said. "He was rescuing me early on but left when Jake showed up."

"Where did he go?"

Sam scanned the page open on her lap. "He went to his office for a while and then home. He says Miss P wasn't there." She looked at her partner. "She stayed with you that night, didn't she?"

Mac nodded. "So, neither of them has an alibi." She chewed on a fingernail.

"No, but without more evidence, a lack of alibi means nothing," Jake said.

"Did you get DNA from them?"

"Not yet. We need the results from Killer's toenails and teeth before we have anything to compare it to."

"It's taking a long time." A dull headache throbbed across Mac's brow. "I think I'll go back to my room for now."

"I'm sure the lab is working on it as fast as they can, Mackenzie." Miss P stood and turned Mac's wheelchair toward the door.

Sam hurried over and hugged her friend. "I'll be down to see you in a minute."

"With any luck, I'll be out of here soon." Mac waved Miss P to a stop. "What room is Mr. Fischer in?"

"I think two fifteen," Alan said.

"I'll stop by before going back to Emergency." Mac glanced up at Miss P. "Okay?"

"Whatever you want, my dear."

As Miss P pushed her down the hall, a doctor came from a room about midway and strode away from her. Dr. Quinn? Same color hair, but she couldn't be sure.

A nurse breezed past them into room two fifteen, Mr. Fischer's room. The sharp sound of alarms seemed to propel her back through the door. "I need a crash team in here stat."

The hospital intercom erupted with "Code blue two fifteen. Code blue two fifteen."

Doctors and nurses materialized from all directions. Miss P maneuvered Mac's chair as close to the opposite wall as she could. Mac inspected every doctor for Quinn. He wasn't one of the responding staff.

Mac stared at the closed door, hands clasped in her lap. Miss P scooted a chair next to her. After what seemed like hours, the door opened, and a doctor stepped into the hallway.

"One of you wouldn't be Mac, would you?" He furrowed his brow.

Unable to speak, she raised a hand.

He crossed the hallway and jammed his hands into his scrub's pockets. "Mr. Fischer had a heart attack. We got to him in time."

Mac let out the breath she'd been holding. "Thank God."

"Before he lost consciousness, he kept mumbling something like—Tell Mac he knows." The doctor shrugged. "I assume you understand what he was talking about."

"I think so." And if she was right, she needed to get back to her office as soon as possible. "Thanks, doctor." She jumped from her wheelchair. Her cracked ribs protested at the sudden activity, and she grabbed Miss P by the hand.

"Hey. What are you doing?" The young man asked.

"I'm fine." She waved at him over her shoulder and realized she still wore a hospital gown. She would need to retrieve her own clothes—after she talked to Jake and Sam again.

She pushed through the door into Jake's room. "Someone tried to murder Mr. Fischer, and I think I know …"

Dr. David Quinn stood next to Jake's bed.

"Mac, there you are." Sam rushed over and gave her a be-quiet look. "Dr. Quinn dropped by to see how Jake was doing."

"What were you saying about Mr. Fischer?" Quinn asked.

"He had a heart attack. Right after you came from his room." She probed his face for any spark of surprise. None. "They stopped it in time."

"That's too bad. But I was never in his room."

Too bad he had the heart attack or too bad they got it stopped in time? Mac wrapped an arm around her hurting ribs. "I would have sworn I saw you leaving his room minutes before the nurse found him."

"It wasn't me." He gave her a look of pity and glanced at his watch. "Good to see you're doing so well, detective. Ladies." He nodded at Sam and her mother. As he passed Mac, he paused. "You really should get some rest, Miss Love."

After Quinn left, Jake ran a hand through his hair. "Mac, what were you thinking? You as much as accused one of our suspects of attempted murder. What if he's the killer, and he comes after you?"

"Listen." Mac raised her hands. "I'm already in the crosshairs. Mr. Fischer told the doctor, 'Tell Mac he knows.'"

"Knows what?" Jake asked. "About Rosa being dead?"

"Yes, and about her will." Mac stopped and faced Sam. "I think he also knows we have the original at the office."

"How?"

"Because Mr. Fischer told him."

"Why would he do that?"

"Either he had no choice, or he thought he could trust him." A wave of sadness passed through Mac. "And he didn't realize his mistake until it was too late."

"What a blessing the nurse walked in when she did, but who would Mr. Fischer trust that much?" Miss P asked.

"People his age—no offense, Miss P—put a lot of trust in their doctors."

"But he knew Dr. Quinn is on our suspect list." Sam furrowed her brow. "I can't see him telling him anything without being coerced."

"Or tricked." Jake's face turned to stone. "Either way, it's done, and I can't stay here any longer."

"Me neither," Mac said. "I'm getting my things from Emergency and heading to the office."

"Mac, wait. Let's talk about this." Sam paced. "The safe at the office is one of the best on the market and well-hidden. Even if they search for it, the chances of them finding it are slim." Sam looked at her brother. "And Jake can put someone outside our office, right? They'd probably get caught before they could do much damage."

"For a couple of nights." He nodded. "Until you can move the will to the bank."

"We all could use some sleep." Sam put an arm around her husband. "Let's go home and regroup in the morning."

"I guess that's okay for tonight." Mac chewed on her thumbnail. "But I plan on being at the office bright and early."

"We all will."

Mac returned to Emergency, changed clothes, and waited outside for Miss P to pick her up. Dr. Quinn came through the double doors and hesitated.

"Miss Love." He took a step closer, hand over his heart.

She inched toward the door.

"I'm not sure why you think I had anything to do with Mr. Fischer's heart attack, but I can assure you, I didn't."

Something in the tone of his voice made her search for his eyes. If she could see them, she'd know if he was telling the truth. He raised his head out of the shadows, and the glow from Miss P's headlights illuminated his face.

Mac took a step back. His eyes shone with sincerity, but they revealed something else to her, and she prayed her expression didn't give it away. He may not have caused Fischer's heart attack, but now she knew who killed Rosa —and why.

If only she could find the proof.

CHAPTER 33

Indian summer was over, and cold air from Canada covered Washington once more. Weak morning light filtered through the clouds. Mac paced between the frosty front window of the office and the conference table, chewing on her fingernail. Where were Sam and Jake? She stopped by her chair and made another note on her pad.

"Please sit down, Mackenzie." Miss P offered her a mug of coffee. "The others will be here soon."

She took the cup in both hands and held it below her nose. The aroma of fresh Columbia blend had to be one of life's greatest pleasures. "Thanks, Miss P."

"Good morning." Sam's lilting voice blew in with a gust of cold air. "I'll take one of those."

"Close the door." Mac shivered, and a drop of coffee sloshed onto her notepad.

"Hello to you too, Madame Grumpy." Sam gave her a quick hug around the shoulders.

Mac smiled despite herself. "Hi, Sam."

"You've been busy." She glanced at Mac's notes. "I'll get my computer and join you.”

“Where’s Jake?”

“He went into the precinct.” Sam plopped into a chair and tapped a few keys. “He’ll be by later.”

Anxiety gnawed at her, and she pushed her coffee mug aside. “I need to talk to him.” Mac ran a finger down her list as she waited for him to answer the phone.

“I only have a few minutes,” Jake said.

“Do you have DNA results from Killer’s nails and teeth?”

“Yes.” The sound of papers being shuffled came through the phone. “And before you ask, I’m getting samples from Nate and the doctor today. In fact, Nate’s due here any minute for an interview.”

“You’re interviewing Nate?” Mac shot a look at Miss P and Sam, who stared in her direction.

“And no, you can’t come,” Jake said in his sternest voice. “I’ll brief you after it’s over.”

“But—” Too late. He’d hung up.

Mac made a check next to Killer’s DNA on her list. One step closer to having the evidence she needed. But oh, how she ached to be a bug, a piece of trash, or even a speck of dust in the room when Jake interviewed Nate.

She read the next notation on her list. “Miss P, have you had any success getting pictures of the new hires at Fischer Industries?”

“Yes.” Their assistant opened a file and passed copies to Mac and Sam. “Of course, you already know Claudia Smith.”

Mac read through her information again and studied her photo. She turned the page. Otis Miller, the new maintenance man. She gripped the page. “He’s the cleaner at the hospital.”

“The one you and Jake saw in Rosa’s room?” Sam asked.

“Yes. He must work in both places.” Mac rubbed her forehead. “We need to check him out.”

"I will take my file to the hospital and make some inquiries," Miss P said.

"And I'll get Jake to do a check." Sam made a note.

The other files held no surprises, and Mac marked photos of hires off her list. A ribbon of excitement twirled inside her as she moved down her list. She was closing in on him.

"Shall we talk about the Lombardi Company?" Miss P moved a slim folder in front of her. "I was able to find out what the latest vote is about."

Mac snorted. "I'd love to hear why the man tried to kidnap me for a second time."

"As you know, the Lombardi Company is named after Rosa's family. Rosa is the CEO, while her father, Robert Genovese, is the COO of the company. Rosa's mother kept her maiden name and gave it to her daughter, apparently."

"I imagine that didn't go over too well with her husband," Mac said.

"I'm sure it didn't. And of course, he brought in the foreign investors, which have proven to be a thorn in his side as well." Miss P pushed her glasses up her nose. "He has a chance to divest himself of them, but of course, he needs Rosa's vote to do so." She peered at Mac. "Which is why he concocted his little scheme to kidnap you and have you pose as Rosa."

"Sorry, Robert." Mac wiped away a mock tear.

"Indeed."

"Mac, did you find out anything interesting about the company from Fischer's file?" Sam asked.

"No. Most of the information was too old and related to business transactions. Nothing personal."

"There was one item I ran across that seemed odd." Miss P withdrew a news article from twenty years ago. "Mr. Genovese was at a news conference about—"

The front door opened, and chilled air fluttered the papers

on the table.

"May I come in?" Claudia Smith stood on the mat, wrapped in an elegant cloak.

Jake held the door for Nate. "Thanks for coming, Mr. Westcott." He indicated the chair to the left of the door and took a seat with his back to the camera.

"Is this an interview, detective, or an interrogation?" Nate crossed his ankles. One knee bounced, then stilled.

Jake scratched a note on his pad. It was a reminder to get cat food, but Nate didn't know that, and writing made people nervous. He wanted Nate nervous.

"No," Jake said. "I need your help with a few things."

"Okay."

"I understand you work for Rosa's father."

Nate glanced at the camera above Jake's head. "Are you recording this interview?"

"Yes."

"Then no comment."

"Mr. Westcott, I can assure you what you say here stays here."

"Sorry, detective, but I've heard that before. Either you shut down the camera, or this interview is over." Nate stood.

Jake faced the camera and ran a finger across his throat.

Nate waited for the red light to blink out before regaining his seat.

"Do you mind if I take notes?" Jake asked.

"I guess not."

"Back to my question. Do you work for Rosa's father?"

"Yes."

"What are you doing in Washington, Missouri?"

"I came to find Rosa. She disappeared, and we believed she'd try to contact Mr. Fischer."

"Is the rest of your story true? Are you Miss P's nephew, and did you date Miss Love in college?"

"Yes." Nate leaned his elbows on his knees and clasped his hands. "I know you care about Mac, and so do I. I wouldn't do anything to hurt her."

Jake stared at his pad. "Except lie to her and let her get kidnapped." He raised his eyes to Nate's. "You knew she looked exactly like Rosa, and yet you let her go through all the trauma of being held captive."

"I didn't—" Nate surged to his feet, his hands clenched, and his eyes darkened with anger.

"Sit. Down." Jake's voice boomed in the small space.

The man across from him sank into his chair as if his legs would no longer hold him. He lowered his head into his hands and murmured words Jake couldn't make out.

"Look at me." The detective studied the face of the other man. "Did you play a part in Mac's kidnapping?"

Nate stared at him for a long moment. "I knew they wouldn't hurt her, and I called it off before they could take her away."

"You orchestrated the kidnapping?" It was all Jake could do to stay in his chair.

"Under orders from her father. He thought she was Rosa."

"Because you told him so."

"No. His thugs did. I let them believe it." Nate held up his hands. "I tried to throw the real bad guys off the scent, so I had more time to find Rosa. You understand, don't you? You were there when I rescued Mac."

"But your scheme backfired, didn't it?" Jake jumped to his feet. "Wait here." If he didn't get out of the room, he'd strangle the man.

CHAPTER 34

Mac rose and placed a hand on her aching ribs. "Miss Smith, have a seat." She'd forgotten about Fischer's assistant. Another set of questions she'd wanted to add to her list.

"Ladies, I made some soup." Miss P stood. "Why don't I get us some with homemade bread for an early lunch?"

"I'll help." Sam popped up and followed the older woman to the kitchen.

"I feel like I interrupted something." Smith removed her cloak and gloves.

Mac admired women who could make the most ordinary motions look elegant. Claudia Smith was one of those women.

"We were going over some details for a case." Mac pointed to her notepad.

"Mr. Fischer's case?"

"No, another one, but he's involved in it, too."

Claudia gave a slow nod of her head. "The Rosa Lombardi case."

"How do you know about the Lombardi case?" Mac asked.

"In fact, why don't you tell me who you really are." She made it a statement, not a question. She was tired of all the deception.

"You're very good, Mac." Claudia smiled at her. "No, I'm not a professional assistant by trade. I'm undercover for Homeland Security."

Mac's mouth fell open.

Miss P and Sam entered with lunch. "Close your mouth, dear. It's very unbecoming."

Claudia laughed. "It's my fault. I told her the truth about who I am—an undercover agent for Homeland Security."

Sam dropped her spoon in her soup. "You have got to be kidding."

Claudia shook her head.

Miss P carved the bread into thick slices without missing a stroke.

"You don't seem surprised, Miss P?"

"At my age, Miss Smith, it's very hard to surprise me." She offered the plate of fresh bread to the agent. "I imagine you're at Fischer Industries because Mr. Fischer has bid on the contract with Boeing."

"Yes." Claudia Smith's eyes widened. "How did you know?"

"It's a federal contract, I presume, and so the government would want to check on any companies before getting involved." Miss P peered at her over her glasses. "Are you investigating Mr. Fischer's current problem?"

"I've solved that one. It was the maintenance man, Otis Miller."

Mac wiped her mouth and shuffled through the papers beside her. "Is this the man you're talking about?" She handed Miller's file to Smith.

"Yes, that's him. Our agents should be taking him into custody as we speak."

"Do you think he was responsible for the glue on the steps?"

"I'm certain of it."

"You still haven't said how you know about the Rosa Lombardi case."

"I bugged Mr. Fischer's office."

"You must have heard him say he didn't trust you." Sam cringed. "I'm sure he didn't mean it."

"It's okay." Claudia smiled. "I almost got caught at your party."

"I wondered about that." Mac set her glass down and focused on Claudia. "Who was it that spooked you?"

"Mrs. Sanders, Jake and Sam's mother."

"My mother?" Sam choked on her drink. "How do you know my mother?"

"Your mother and my mother live next door to each other in Florida. They're friends. I've met your mom a time or two when I was there on a visit."

"What a small world." A smile lifted the corners of Mac's mouth.

The phone rang, and Sam answered. "Mackenzie Love and Samantha Majors, Private Investigators." Her face lit up. "Alan. Why are you calling on this phone?"

She held up her hand. "Let me put you on speaker."

"I found something in Mac's old newsletters you might be interested in."

"What?" Mac asked.

"Nate got married. I'll read you what it says. 'We heard from a reliable source Nathanial Xander Westcott III married into a very influential Chicago business family this past weekend.'"

"That's all it says?"

"Yes."

"Take pictures of the front of the newsletter and of the column, and text them to me," Mac said. "Good work, Alan. Keep this up, and we may have to put you on the payroll."

"Bye, sweetheart." Samantha pressed End. Her face glowed with pride.

Mac's phone dinged. She studied the images before passing it to Sam. Nate married to Rosa? But if that were true, he must have known how close she and his wife resembled each other.

"I need to get these to Jake before he's done with Nate's interview." Mac pressed the Send arrow. The door flew open. Cold air hit her back. Had to be Jake. Too late. "Wait till you hear what we found out."

But the look on Sam's face told a different story. Mac bolted from her seat. Her peripheral vision caught Claudia Smith as she rose from her chair, a pistol in her hand.

Dr. Quinn stepped into the light and slammed the door. He pointed a gun at the group of women.

"Federal Agent." Smith's voice sounded like steel. "Put the gun down."

To Mac's surprise, Quinn swiveled the barrel and shot. Smith's gun fired beside her with a deafening roar. Her shot went high. Plaster from the ceiling rained on Quinn. Gun smoke and dust filled the air, and Claudia Smith crumbled to the floor.

"You shot her." Sam burst from her chair and rounded the table. "You're a doctor. How could you?" She grabbed napkins from the table and pressed them against the wound.

"I wasn't about to give her my gun." His voice cut through the air like a scalpel. "Sit down, Mac. We need to have a little talk."

Mac willed Sam to look at her. Claudia's handgun lay inches from Sam's knee. If she could get hold of it ...

Quinn strolled over and kicked the weapon across the room under the couch. So much for that idea.

"What do you want to talk about?"

"How about wills? Rosa's in particular."

"I don't know anything about Rosa's will." *Lord, You are my strength and my shield.*

"Don't play games with me, Mackenzie Love." He moved behind Miss P. "I don't play well with others. Never have. That's why Mama sent me away."

"Is that what they told you? Your mama sent you away?" Mac's stomach clenched. She had to keep him talking, give Jake time to get here. "And you've lived your whole life believing your mother didn't love you."

"Yes." He gave her a quizzical look. "What do you know?"

She placed a finger beside her nose. "I know things."

"Like what?"

"Like you're Rosa's twin. You both have one blue eye and one brown."

He raised his free hand to his face. "My contact lens fell out. That's easy to figure out. What else do you know?"

"Like they lied to you. The reason you were sent to live with them was because your father didn't want you." Mac stared at him. "He told your mama to get rid of you."

"Robert?" His face sagged. "Is he my real father?"

"Yes." Real father? Were Rosa and David the product of an affair?

"But Robert and I are going to run the company together. He promised." His eyes pleaded with her to take back what she'd said.

The little boy still searching for love and acceptance. She glanced at Sam to see if she heard all of this. Sam gave a slight nod. Miss P shifted her body in slow movements to the left. Mac caught sight of the bread knife in her lap.

JAKE LEANED against the wall and took a few deep breaths. Chief Baker marched across the hall and stood in front of him.

"You're too close to this one, son."

"Chief, I can do this." Jake held up a hand. "Give me time to calm down."

"You can watch, but I'm putting Detective Walker in." The Chief waved a hand to the detective standing a few feet away.

"Sorry, man." Walker squeezed Jake's shoulder as he passed.

Jake hurried to his room and switched his computer on to watch the interview. The screen was black. He'd told them to stop filming. Wait. The interview room had a two-way mirror. They hadn't used it in years, but it was still in place. He made it there in time to see Walker finish introducing himself to Nate.

"What happened to Detective Sanders?" Nate scratched his ear.

"He got called away on another case." Walker read over Jake's notes. "How well did you know Rosa Lombardi?"

Nate folded his arms across his chest and looked at his shoes.

"Do you want me to repeat what I said?"

"I heard you. I'm trying to decide how to answer."

"What's so hard about the question?"

Nate barked a laugh. "You have no idea."

"Then fill me in."

In the viewing room, Jake's phone pinged. He glanced at the text from Mac. His eyes caught on Nate's name, and he enlarged the image. He yanked the door open and ran out of the viewing room before Nate answered.

"We're in the process of getting a divorce."

The interview room was locked. He banged on the door.

"Excuse me." Watkins walked to the door. "Go away, Sanders," Watkins growled at him.

"Please, let me sit in with you. I promise not to say a thing."

"If you do, I'll throw you out and go straight to the Chief."

"I understand."

Watkins let him in and placed the extra chair next to his. "Not a peep," he said under his breath.

Jake nodded.

"I guess you're finished with your other case," Nate said.

"I'm conducting this interview, Mr. Westcott. You will address your statements and questions to me, please." Watkins gave Jake a sideways glare.

"Yes, sir."

"Back to your marriage to Rosa Lombardi. How long did it last?"

"Not long. A couple of years. We both married for the wrong reasons."

The marriage was over? Jake opened his mouth to ask what he'd missed, but snapped it shut again.

"I can guess why you married her. She'd be a wealthy woman after her father died."

"That's not why." Nate glared at him. "But it was still not right. I married her because she reminded me of someone else." He glanced at Jake.

Nate married Rosa because she looked like Mac. But he found out that wasn't good enough. *There's only one Mackenzie Love in the world.* Something like pity touched Jake's heart.

"I don't care about Rosa's shares. I'm a lawyer, not a businessman. But there is someone else who'd like to get his hands on her share of the company."

"Who?" Jake asked, his promise to be silent forgotten.

"Her brother." Anger dripped from Nate's tone.

CHAPTER 35

Jake looked askance at Detective Watkins, who nodded his assent. "I never heard about a brother. Who is he?"

"He's her twin. Their mother had an affair, and she got pregnant. She and her lover agreed she'd keep Rosa, and he would get the son." Nate's gaze unfocused, as if he were remembering a scene from the past. "Rosa never knew. Neither did Robert, her stepfather. He was out of the country when they were born, and he thought Rosa was his. It wasn't until recently he found out there was a boy too. He was so upset."

"Did he hunt for the boy—man now?"

"Yes, and he found him." Nate blinked. "I never met him. By then, Rosa and I were separated, and I was persona non grata at her the house. But I heard stories about how she was frightened of her brother, and I believe that's why she left."

Fraternal twins. A girl and a boy. They don't have to look anything alike. Or they could have a common trait. "Do you know his name, or where we can find a picture of him?"

Nate shook his head. "I wish I did."

Watkins looked at Jake. "Any more questions?"

"No."

"Nathanial Xander Westcott III, I'm arresting you in connection with the kidnapping of Mackenzie Love." Detective Watkins opened the door and waved an officer inside. "This officer will read you your rights and escort you to a holding cell." He waited for Jake to pass through the doorway into the hall. "Come on, Jake."

Once outside the interview room, Jake stopped. "Watkins, have you ever worn contact lenses?"

The detective cocked a questioning eyebrow at Jake. "No. Why?"

"You can change your eye color with those things, can't you?"

"Sure can. More than one bad guy has used them in a disguise. What are you thinking, Jake?"

"About how easy it would be to hide one blue eye and one brown." An urgent desire to see Mac washed over him. "I've got to go."

"What about the Chief? We need to give him our report."

"Tell him Mac's done it again, and I'll need back-up at her office. He'll know what I mean."

"Robert must regret what he did." Mac forced herself to smile at Quinn. "You're a successful doctor now. He would want to make up for all those years."

"That's what he said." Quinn straightened. "But first I needed to get Rosa's shares, and the way to do it was to kill her and get rid of her will." He narrowed his eyes at Mac. "Being her next closest blood relative, I would inherit her shares."

"Why didn't you ask Rosa if she'd give you an interest in the company?"

"I did." He advanced on her. "Do you think I'm stupid? She said no."

Mac sprang to her feet. Her chair toppled backwards. Once more, a gun was pointed at her chest.

Miss P raised her hand and sliced the sharp bread knife through the flesh in the doctor's right arm. He howled and swung his arm around, knocking her to the ground. Blood showered the table and Sam's computer.

Mac dove to her right and crawled to the couch. Where had Claudia's gun landed? She pressed her stomach to the floor and stretched her arm under as far as it would go. *Lord, help me.* Her fingers touched something cold and hard. She pulled the gun out and pivoted to a seated position, ready to fire.

"I wouldn't if I were you." Quinn stood behind Sam with his weapon pointed at her head. "Put the gun down and get over here. It's time you got me the will."

There would be no more talk. Mac glanced at Miss P. She lay still on the floor.

Quinn took off his shirt and wrapped it around his arm. He noticed the direction of Mac's look. "The old witch," he mumbled.

"How's Claudia?" Mac asked.

"She'll live."

"You shot her. She needs a ... she needs help." She'd almost said a doctor.

"After you get me the will."

Mac reached for her purse, tugged the envelope out, and handed it to him.

He shoved Sam into a chair and secured her hands and feet before flipping the document open and glancing at it. "This is a copy. I need the original."

"It's in my safe deposit box at the bank."

Quinn came toe-to-toe with her and studied her face.

She stared back, stone-faced.

"You're good." His warm breath prickled her skin. "But Fischer told me you put it in your safe here." He placed the barrel of his gun under her chin. "Get it."

Mac narrowed her eyes at him. Without his gun, she was sure she could take him. Cold anger settled in the pit of her stomach. She despised bullies.

"Move."

Mac led the way to her office. "After you have the will, you'll have to kill us."

"Yes."

"Tell me, why should I get it for you?" Mac crossed her arms.

"Because if you do, I'll kill you first, and you won't have to see your friends die."

"I have a better idea. How about I give you the will and you go away and leave us alone?" She took a small step back.

"You forget I shot a federal agent."

"There is that." Mac shifted her stance. "Unfortunate for you." Reaching behind her, she picked up her paperweight.

"Stop stalling or I'll drag one of your ladies in here and—"

Mac threw the paperweight into the air. Quinn instinctively twisted his head to follow its trajectory. For an instant, his guard was down, and that was all Mac needed. She delivered a swift sidekick to his ribs, followed by one to his chin.

Quinn cried out. His gun dropped from his hand as he stumbled back through the doorway into the common room. He headed for the couch and Claudia's gun laying on the floor nearby.

Sirens screamed to a stop in front of the office. The sounds of slamming doors and men pounding up the yard filled Mac with glorious happiness.

Quinn glared at her. "We're not done." He raced through the back door and disappeared.

"Mac. Sam." Jake flung the door open and charged into the room. His brain struggled to make sense of what he was seeing. He keyed his phone. "We need a couple of ambulances." His eyes lit on Mac standing in the doorway to her office, and his heart lurched in his chest.

She met him halfway across the room. "It was ..."

"I know. The doctor."

Mac nodded. She cleared her throat. "Miss P cut him with a bread knife."

"Did she?" Jake looked to where a couple of officers had Miss P sitting in a chair.

"He shot Claudia Smith."

"I can see. An ambulance is on its way."

"Sam ..." Mac choked on her words.

"I'm okay, Mac." Sam hugged her. "We're all going to be okay."

"He got away." She flashed into a sudden fury.

"We'll get him." Jake turned her face to his so she could read the promise there. "We've got his car. He's on foot. He won't get far that way."

The blood drained from her face. "What time is it?"

"Almost four."

"He's headed for Ivy."

CHAPTER 36

Awhisper of terror ran through Mac, building with every ring of her phone. "Pick up, Ivy." But her call went to voicemail.

"I've sent a squad car over to Cowan's to catch her before she leaves."

Mac paced the room, her mind unable to focus on anything but her old friend. *I beg you, Lord, protect her.*

Alan and the ambulance arrived at the same time.

"Sam, would you and Alan take Miss P to the hospital?" Mac asked.

"I'm fine." Miss P held up her hand in protest.

"It's good business to make sure our employees are cared for."

"True." She pushed her glasses up her nose and accepted Alan's proffered arm.

Mac breathed a sigh of relief. Three of her cherished people would be out of harm's way for a while. Once the EMTs moved Claudia Smith out of the office and into the ambulance, she would be free to concentrate on Ivy.

"Bad news." Jake joined her at the front window. "Her boss says Ivy got a call and asked to leave early. She said it was an emergency."

"We need to get out there and search for her." Mac yanked her coat from the hall tree. "She drives a green hatchback with a peace symbol on the rear bumper."

"Hang on." Jake put a hand on her arm. "Washington may not be a big city, but it's not small. They could be anywhere. I say we wait a bit."

"For what?"

"My men are patrolling. If they spot them, they'll call me. Besides, I have a hunch the doc still believes he can get his hands on the will."

Mac scrunched up her face. "That's nuts."

"I agree, but he's not thinking straight right now, is he?"

"No." Mac eased out of her coat and hung it back up. She entered her office and opened the safe. "Amazing what havoc a few sheets of paper can cause." She held up the will.

"You're not going to turn it over to him, are you?" Jake's eyes widened.

"No. I'm going to use the original envelope and the copied will. I'll seal it with wax and pray it works long enough to rescue Ivy and catch the monster who has her." If she got the chance to try her trick.

Mac laid the envelope on a chair and walked over to the conference table. Blood spatter told the tale of what happened that afternoon, and it wasn't pretty. She went into the kitchen and returned with a cloth and some spray.

"Stop. The forensics guys have to do their thing first, Mac."

"I can't wipe off Sam's computer?"

"Sorry." He took the rag and can from her hands. "We'll make sure it gets cleaned like new."

"Can I at least get my papers? There's no blood on them."

Irritation sharpened her tone, but she couldn't help it. She hated having to wait.

"I guess."

But when she reached for them, her hands trembled. She needed to sit for a minute. She collapsed on the sofa and wrapped herself in a fierce hug. Scenes from this afternoon rushed at her like daytime nightmares.

With a suddenness that took her breath away, the scene changed to the interior of a car. She couldn't see over the front seat. Beth was next to her. Her sister was screaming. The car swerved, and she tumbled to the floor.

"Mac?" Jake stepped closer. "Are you okay?"

She shook her head, unable to speak.

He sat and pulled her into his embrace. "I've got you."

She laid her ear against his chest. The steady beat of his heart and the warmth radiating off his body worked together to dispel the visions. She let out a sigh of relief and sat up.

"What happened?" Jake rubbed her shoulder.

"I'm worried about Ivy." She ran a shaky hand over her forehead.

"It looked like more than that to me."

"Well, it wasn't. I need a drink of water." She headed for the kitchen. "Want some?"

"Yes."

The last set of visions left her more confused than ever. No doubt they were memories dredged from her childhood. But of what? And why were they surfacing now? She had no intention of sharing this knowledge with Jake. Not while her long-time friend could be riding around with a killer. She snagged two water bottles and returned to the large common room.

"Where?" Jake stood, his phone clamped to his ear. "Got it." He raised his eyes to hers. "Ivy's car's been spotted going toward the river on Lafayette."

Mac dropped the water bottles on the conference table and ran for the front door. She snatched her purse and coat on the way. Jake charged after her. In his SUV, he switched his radio to speaker in order to follow the pursuit.

"He's heading for the park," the officer said.

"He could take a boat." Fear closed about her throat like a hand. "Ivy can't swim."

"Train coming from the east. We got him." A second of relief over the radio. "He's going around the barriers." The officer uttered a curse that got lost in a hideous screech of the train's emergency brakes.

A train horn blasted in stereo—one from the radio and one from outside as Mac and Jake neared the intersection. She stared in horror as two great orange giants yelling like banshees passed her. After what seemed like hours, the shrieking beast came to a shuddering stop—the last ten box cars blocking the intersection. Ivy's car had made it through, but the train blocked their access.

"We need to get this train off the crossing." Jake yelled to his men.

"I'm sorry, sir, but the engineer said they have to restore the air pressure in the brakes before they can move again."

"How long does it take?"

"About ten minutes? Also, they need to walk the train and make sure the connections are okay."

Jake thrust a hand through his hair.

Mac took off running east on Front Street. Ivy's smiling face filled her mind. David Quinn was a walking dead man.

"Stop."

Jake's commanding voice barely registered among her anxious thoughts. The sound of several pairs of feet pounding after her spurred her on. The condos on her right shed enough light on the street for her to see where she was going. Until she reached the end of the pavement. She ran into the grass without breaking stride.

"Mac. Stop."

The end of the train came into view, and she veered left. She caught sight of Jake. He was gaining on her. Digging deep, she increased her pace.

"Hey. You can't be here." Two men with flashlights shone them in her direction. "You're trespassing. This is railroad property."

Mac hopscotched over the tracks and slid down the stone embankment.

"This is railroad property." The man screamed again.

"Police." Jake yelled.

Where was the gap in the fence? She'd been a kid the last time she'd used it. Mac strained to see in the low light. There it was. She slipped through and picked up her pace again.

As she ran past the old waterworks building, the train started to move, and by the time she made it across Lafayette Street, the crossing was clear. Police cars streamed into the park. She ignored them and focused on Ivy's green hatchback sitting in the lower parking lot.

"Mac, don't." Jake caught her as she reached the car. "Let the police take care of this."

She fought to break his hold on her without success. "I need to know if Ivy's in the car."

"You can watch from here."

The officers opened all the doors and the hatch. No sign of her friend. Another officer jogged over to where Jake and Mac were standing.

"Sir, a man saw the suspect take a boat and head out into the river."

"I need to speak to him." Jake took off after the officer, and Mac followed.

An unshaven man in dirty clothes sat on a bench next to another police officer.

"Tell Detective Sanders what you told me."

The man scrubbed a hand down his chin. "I was minding my own business when the train took to screeching and blowing its horn like to wake the devil. I looked up and seen a green car come around the gates in front of the treain." The man pressed a hand to his chest. "'bout gave me a heart attack."

"What happened then?"

"It raced down to the bottom parking lot, and a guy jumped out and ran up the path toward the boats." He pointed toward the docks. "He stole Mr. Kelso's best fishing boat."

"Which way was he headed?"

"That way." The grizzled man pointed downstream. "But he won't get very far."

"Why not?"

"Kelso only keeps a gallon of gas in the tank when he's not using it."

"Was there anyone with the guy?"

"Nay. He was by himself."

Where was Ivy?

"How tall would you say he was?" Jake asked. "About my height?"

"No. He was a short guy."

"What was he wearing?"

"One of those black hoody things."

Jake glanced at her. "You're sure the driver was a man?"

Mac couldn't believe her ears. Did Jake think Ivy drove her car to the park and stole the boat? Impossible.

"I guess it coulda been a woman." The witness puckered his brow. "Come to think of it, he did kind of run like a girl."

A biting wind blew off the river, and Jake put an arm around Mac. "Let's go sit in my patrol car." He expected her to resist, but she didn't. Once inside, he turned the heater on full blast.

"It can't be Ivy. She doesn't like water." Mac spoke as if she were the only one there. "Maybe Quinn had some other girl on the hook, and she helped him." She rubbed her temple. "No. I would have known. Or the witness got it wrong."

"Maybe." Jake joined her conversation. "But the difference between a man my size and a woman Ivy's size is noticeable."

"But why would she help him? I don't get it."

"Me either. Except you told me she fell hard for him. No telling what kind of sob story he fed her."

An officer tapped on the window. "We found the boat about a quarter mile downstream against the bank. Nothing in it except an orange life jacket." The police officer consulted his phone. "They found some shoe prints in the mud. Size 9 woman's sneakers."

"Thanks. Let me know about any other developments. I'm headed to the hospital."

"Yes, sir."

He'd sensed Mac's reaction to the shoe imprint information even before he turned to find her head in her hands. "Buckle up. We need to check on Miss P and Claudia Smith." He would keep her mind off Ivy by putting it on her other friends. At least for now.

Mac sighed and sat up. "Yes.

MAC HUGGED HER RIB CAGE. How many times had she been in the emergency room in the past few years? Too many. She followed Jake through the doors to where Miss P waited to be released.

"I told you I was fine." Her former chemistry teacher sniffed her disdain. "This was a waste of time."

Sam rolled her eyes at Mac over Miss P's head.

"We talked about this before you left. You're a valued member of our team, and we take care of each other." Mac threw a hand up, palm out. "End of discussion."

"We're glad you're okay, Miss P," Jake said. "It's been a rough night for all of us. Where's Claudia Smith?"

"She's in ICU. She's doing okay, but they want to monitor her for a couple of nights," Sam said.

"Have you called her mother?"

"Since she's undercover, Homeland Security said no. Unless she takes a turn for the worse."

"Is her handler with her?"

"They've got someone with her twenty-four/seven. Not sure if he's her handler."

"I need to speak with him." He caught Mac's gaze. "Want to come?"

"Yes." Jake had never invited her along on an official interview before—much less with a Homeland Security agent. She looked at Sam and Miss P.

But a lot had happened, and she owed it to her partners to brief them on where things stood.

"But I'd better stay here and talk to Sam and Miss P." She fixed her face into a positive look to hide her disappointment. "We'll talk later, and you can fill me in."

"I will." He nodded at the others and left the room.

"What happened?" Concern edged Sam's words.

Mac took a deep breath and started with the call from Ivy's boss, letting them know she'd left early. She finished with an apology to Miss P for being so harsh.

"No apology necessary. I was being a stubborn old lady."

"I can't imagine Ivy …" Sam stared at Mac. "You've known her since you were kids."

"Did you have her in chemistry, Miss P?" Alan, who had sat quietly up to now, asked.

"Yes. She was a timid little thing. Not very bright, but sweet."

Misery descended on Mac like a sudden downpour. Her very bones cried out for sleep. "Can you and Alan take Miss P home?"

"She's staying with us tonight." Sam placed an arm around the older woman's shoulders. "I called Mom, and she's fixing a bed in the other spare room for her."

"Good." Mac willed her legs to support her as she stood. "I need to go home and rest."

JAKE HESITATED outside the door to Miss P's room. Should he wait for Mac? She could be a pain, but the truth was he liked working with her on a case. Besides, when she was with him, he didn't have to worry about what she was up to. But who knew how long she'd be talking to her friends. He sighed and headed for the ICU.

A man in khakis and a green polo shirt stood inside the door of Claudia Smith's room. Jake displayed his ID and gestured for him to leave the room.

"Detective Sanders. I wondered when the police would show up." The man offered his hand. "I'm Agent Barstow, but as far as the hospital is concerned, I'm Claudia's brother, John Smith. A female agent and I are staying with Agent Smith until we can move her to a more secure location."

"If you need any help, let me know." Jake gave him a card. "How is Claudia?"

"She'll be okay."

"Will she be able to work as an agent again?"

The man raised one shoulder. "Too soon to tell."

The two men shared a moment of silence. Jake lived each day with the fear of an injury that would prevent him from continuing to do his job. And he imagined the same was true for the Homeland Security agent.

"Has she said anything relevant to my case?" Jake ran a hand through his hair.

"She goes in and out and hasn't said much of anything."

"I understand you've been searching for Otis Miller in connection with the problems at Fischer Industries."

"Yes. We haven't found him, but we will."

"With any luck, he left town."

"I don't think so." Agent Barstow shook his head. "I've seen his type before. It's a matter of pride with them. He'll want to finish the job he came to do."

CHAPTER 38

Mac pressed hang up on her phone without opening her eyes and drifted back to sleep. She'd just gotten to bed. The shrill ring penetrated her dreams again. She grabbed the instrument of torture and threw it across the room.

It continued to ring. Must be important. Maybe an emergency. Mac uncovered her head. Miss P or Sam or one of her sisters. She sat up. Or Jake. The phone stopped ringing. She threw the covers off and hurried over to where her phone lay silent.

It was Jake. With shaky fingers, she pressed redial.

"Are you okay?"

"Yes. We found Ivy."

Mac dropped to the floor. "Is she in custody?"

"Yes. We're about to interview her, and I'd like you to sit in."

"No way." She threw her hand up, palm out.

"Yes way. You're her best friend. She'll talk to you."

A chill traveled up her spine, and her teeth chattered.

"Mac? Are you okay?"

"I'd just gotten to sleep when you called." She cast a wistful look at her snug bed. "I'm too tired to do what you ask."

"Please. We need you." He paused. "I need you."

She closed her eyes and let his voice envelop her like a warm blanket. "Give me half an hour."

"Thank you."

A hot shower, clean clothes, and coffee helped her join the land of the living once more. But she had one more thing to do before leaving. She clicked on the light by the chair in her bedroom. Before confronting Ivy, she needed strength and wisdom. She opened her Bible to some of her favorite verses and prayed to Him, the only source she trusted.

AT THE PRECINCT, Mac exited her car into the brisk wind. A little less than one week until Thanksgiving. She studied the clouds scudding across the moonlit sky. Would it snow this year? She brought her gaze down to the glass doors into the Public Safety building. An even more important question was would her childhood friend be spending the holiday in jail?

"Mac." Jake appeared at the entrance. "Thanks for coming."

Her heart reacted with a spark of joy to his voice, followed by irritation. "Did I have a choice?"

He led the way up the stairs to the police station.

"Sorry," she said to his back. "I'm tired."

"I get it. It's okay." At the top, he turned and gave her one of his smiles—the kind that made her stomach flip. "I know this is hard for you."

She nodded, unable to speak.

At the interview room door, he hesitated. "So far, Ivy hasn't said a thing. She doesn't know you're coming. I'm hoping you'll be able to get her talking."

He opened the door and let Mac go in ahead of him.

"Mac, what are you doing here?" Ivy jumped up from her chair to the left of the door.

The two friends hugged, and Mac pulled away. She took the chair Jake offered facing Ivy. "Please tell me this is all a big mistake. Tell me you didn't help David Quinn escape." Mac ached to reach out to her friend but didn't.

"I get it now." Ivy pushed back in her chair. "They're using you to get me to talk." She glared at Jake.

"They're not using me, Ivy. I wanted to come." Unbidden, tears tracked down Mac's face. "We've been through a lot together. I thought I knew you, but this ..."

"Please don't, Mac." Ivy buried her face in her hands. "I can stand anything but seeing you cry."

"I can't help it. Why would you risk so much for this man?"

"You wouldn't understand." The redhead dropped her hands and glared at Mac. "You've never had trouble getting a boyfriend. Right now, you've got two men chasing you—Jake and that lawyer, Nate. It wasn't the same with me."

Oh, Ivy, if you knew. One doesn't know if he wants a relationship, and the other is in this very jail. Mac forced her thoughts back to the woman in front of her.

"What are you talking about? You're beautiful."

"To you, but do you remember the last time I seriously dated someone?" Ivy raised a hand. "Don't bother. You won't be able to. Then along comes David Quinn—Doctor David Quinn. And he loves me."

Mac's friend's face transformed. Her eyes brightened, and her skin glowed. Jake was right. "You did it for love."

"And because they had cheated him out of his inheritance."

"Is that what he told you?"

"Yes, and I believe him." Ivy raised her chin defiantly.

"Did he also tell you he killed Rosa Lombardi? And when he called you, he was running from my office where he'd held Sam, Miss P, and myself hostage after shooting Claudia Smith?"

Ivy's eyes dulled, and her cheeks paled. "I don't believe it."

"It's the truth, Miss Baker," Jake said. "We got a revised autopsy on Rosa Lombardi."

"And I was there when Quinn burst into our office and shot Smith."

"What have I done?" Ivy wrapped her arms around her waist and rocked back and forth in her chair. "How could I have been so stupid? I should have realized nobody would love me like that."

Mac couldn't stay still any longer. She rushed over to her friend and bundled her in her arms. "Don't say those things. You're a vibrant, beautiful woman who trusts people. The jerk took advantage of you, and believe me, he'll pay for it."

"Tell us where he is, Ivy." Jake's words sounded warm and full of concern.

"He stole a car from the parking lot by Cowans and drove north. I think he was headed for his aunt's—if he really has an aunt—in St. Louis."

"Can you describe the car?"

"It was Mr. Jackson's car." Ivy wailed anew. "I'll lose my job. What will I do?"

"One step at a time." Mac stroked her back. "Don't worry about the future. Let's deal with today's problems."

Yeah, Dr. Quinn was today's problem, and they were one step closer to finding him. Jake turned and stepped out of the room.

Jake put a BOLO out on a silver luxury sedan listed to Robert Jackson, driven by a man fitting David Quinn's description. Mac had done the trick. He glanced down the hall toward the interview room.

But it hadn't been a trick. Her desire to get at the truth had been genuine. That's what worked. And that's what he loved about her—one thing—her sincerity.

"Sanders." The Chief's voice cut through his thoughts. "In my office."

"Sir." Jake stepped in and closed the door.

"I've tried to stay away from what's going on down the hall." The balding man placed his folded hands on his desk. "Sit down, Jake. I don't know if you realize Ivy's my niece. My brother's girl."

"No sir. I didn't know." Ivy Baker. Jake did a mental head slap.

"She's a sweet girl, but naïve." The Chief squinted in Jake's direction. "What has she done?"

"I'm afraid she helped a murderer get away." Jake waited for the explosion.

The Chief placed his head in his hands.

"In her defense, the man conned her into believing he loved her and that he was the victim of abuse."

"Do you think she's telling the truth?"

"Yes. She fell apart after we—Mackenzie Love and I told her the truth," Jake said. "Poor kid. Her self-esteem is in the tank. Mac is with her now, trying to make her see it was the jerk's fault, not hers."

"Was she able to help in any way?"

"She told us about the car he stole and where he was headed. I put out a BOLO as soon as I heard."

"Good." The Chief sighed. "I guess I'll have to call my brother and sister-in-law."

Jake kept his eyes averted. No way did he want that job.

"Do me a favor and don't charge her until morning."

"Yes, sir." As Jake left the office, he glanced at the balding man behind the desk. His boss had always been a stickler for following the rules, and that's what he'd taught Jake. Now he was asking him to bend the rules. He had a bad feeling about this.

CHAPTER 39

Mac rinsed her oatmeal bowl and put it in the dishwasher with the other three bowls, five mugs, and assorted eating utensils from this week. A pinch of loneliness hit her at the sight of her meager collection of dirty dishes. She closed the door firmly and walked away.

No time for self-pity. She had work to do. First, she needed to check on her partners.

"Sam, how are you and Miss P doing?"

"We're fine. Mom made us breakfast. Why don't you come over?"

"I had mine. Thanks." Mac walked to the front window. No more police parked outside her house. "Can we meet at the office for a while?"

"Sure, but I'd like to be home by afternoon so I can spend time with Mom."

"Of course." Another stab of pain. Nobody cared if she had time to spend with them.

She hung up and stomped back to her bedroom. Where

was this poor me attitude coming from? She had a good life with lots of friends and family a short drive away. Just because her closest friend since grade school was in jail ... She yanked her brush through her hair. "Ouch."

The physical pain broke through the heart pain, and tears streamed down her cheeks. Ivy was in jail, and not only that, she harbored envy toward Mac. Ivy never let it show, and Mac never picked up on it. What kind of friend did that make her?

Mac dried her eyes and finished getting ready. As she passed the chair in her bedroom, she felt the draw once more. She sat and opened her Bible.

After a time, she rose, ready to face the day. She hoped.

Miss P's large sedan and Sam's mid-sized SUV were both parked at the office when Mac arrived. The enticing aroma of brewing coffee wafted through the door as she stepped inside. "Honey, I'm home."

"It's about time." Sam smiled, taking the sting from her words.

"You can't have been here long." Mac chuckled. "The coffee's still perking."

Miss P joined them from the kitchen. "It should be ready any moment. How are you, Mackenzie?"

"Peachy." Mac examined her friend's face, her old skin swollen and bruised where Quinn hit her. "I'm so sorry."

"Pfft. This is nothing." Miss P waved her sympathy away. "It will heal."

Mac turned her attention to the table and Sam's computer. "Did either of you clean up the blood?"

"No. It was like this when we got here."

"The forensics guys must have. Not usually their job." Mac

surveyed the rest of the room. Where was the envelope with the copy of Rosa's will? "Have you seen a white envelope anywhere?"

Both women shook their heads.

Mac peered under the couch and chairs. Nothing. Would the team last night have taken it as evidence? Her pulse beat faster as she hurried into her office to check the safe. The envelope sat in the middle of her desk, and she breathed a sigh of relief.

"Have I missed anything?" Jake's deep voice came from the other room.

Mac slid the envelope into the top drawer of her desk and joined them. "You're right on time."

As the friends gathered once more around the big table, Mac's heart filled with joy. She leafed through her notepad to a clean page and prepared to write. Sam opened her laptop. and Miss P straightened her stacks of files. Jake placed his phone on the table in front of him.

"Where should we begin?"

"Let's start with how you knew David Quinn was Rosa's brother," Sam said.

"You know the night Jake was in the hospital and you guys got mad at me for accusing Quinn of attempted murder to his face?"

"Yes, and look what happened."

"When I was waiting for Miss P outside the door to the hospital, Quinn approached me. He tried to convince me he wouldn't do such a thing. But when Miss P's headlights shined on his face, I saw he had one blue eye and one brown."

"Like Rosa."

"Exactly. I knew who he really was, and that he had the best reason to kill Rosa."

"I learned Rosa had a brother from Nate," Jake said. "He

told us Rosa's mother had an affair with her doctor and had twins. They agreed Rosa would stay with the mother and the son would live with the father, Dr. Quinn Sr."

"And Rosa's stepfather, Robert Genovese, knew nothing about the affair until a few years ago. He tracked down David Quinn and offered to take him into the business."

"Which is why he killed his sister. And why he showed up here to get her will. To make sure he inherited her shares." Sam shared a look with Miss P. "In the process, Claudia Smith got shot, and he hurt Miss P."

"What will happen to Nate?" Mac asked.

Jake cleared his throat. "We charged Nate as an accessory to kidnapping."

Miss P made a small mewing sound.

"I'm sorry, Miss P," Jake said. "But he works for Rosa's stepfather, and he knowingly let the thugs kidnap Mac to buy time until he could find Rosa himself."

"So, her stepfather ordered the kidnapping and Nate was supposed to help him, but he didn't trust Genovese?" Mac wrinkled her brow. "Is that why Nate sent the text to the head kidnapper about taking my picture and stopped the whole thing? I was a decoy to buy time."

"Yes." Jake's face turned to stone. "And he's lucky you weren't hurt in the process or ..." He took a deep breath. "Is the coffee ready?"

"Of course." Miss P pushed her chair back.

"I'll get it." Sam jumped up and left the room. "Don't say anything major while I'm gone."

Mugs of steaming brew were distributed, and Sam sat once more before her laptop.

"Nate is, or was, in the process of divorcing Rosa—"

"We thought she was the one he married." Mac slapped the

table. "Alan found an article in my old newspapers from college, but it didn't give any names. Anything else on Nate?"

"Unfortunately, we'll have to turn him over to the Feds for further prosecution since he claims his orders came from Chicago."

"Oh Nathanial." Miss P pressed a hand to her heart. "I'm glad my dear sister isn't here to see this."

"If he helps bring Rosa's stepfather to justice, he could get a reduced sentence."

"I will pray he has the good sense to help the authorities."

"So will I, Miss P," Sam said.

"And me." Mac let a moment of silence descend over the group. "Jake, what did you learn from the Homeland Security people?"

"Not much." He took a sip of his coffee. "Claudia Smith wasn't coherent, and they planned on moving her to a secure location as soon as they could. The only thing of interest was they hadn't found Otis Miller, but the agent I spoke to believes he's still in the area."

"Why would he stay?"

"He said guys like him are determined to finish what they start."

Anxiety slithered down Mac's spine. "Where's Mr. Fischer?"

"Do you think Miller might go after him?"

"He tried once. At least that's what Claudia thought." Mac punched a number into her phone. "And if the agents think the guy is still dangerous, then—"

"I can't come to the phone right now," the recorded voice said. "But if you'll leave a message, I'll get back to you."

She waited for the beep. "This is Mackenzie Love. It's urgent. Call me as soon as you get this message." She pressed End. "I don't like this."

"He may be in the bathroom. Or the shower," Sam said. "Give him time to call you back."

"I guess. Anything else, Jake?"

"We're got Ivy in custody but haven't charged her yet per request from the Chief." He wouldn't meet her eyes. "I think it's a bad idea."

"Why?" Mac shot a sour look at Jake.

"It's not going to look good for either the Chief or for her." Jake parried her look with one of his own. "She's in limbo right now. Vulnerable. She'd be better off if things moved forward, and she didn't have time to stew."

He had a point. Last night, she left Ivy on unsteady ground and prayed a good night's sleep would help. "How is she today?"

"I haven't seen her."

"Can you call?"

He pushed a number. "This is Detective Sanders. I'm checking on a prisoner. Ivy Baker." He got up and turned away from the group. "She what? How is she?"

Mac rose and went to his side. She clasped a hand to her roiling stomach.

"Thanks. I'll check on her at the hospital."

Hospital? Mac stiffened.

Jake locked eyes with Mac. "Ivy tried to commit suicide last night."

Mac drew in a breath.

"The guard found her in time, and she's at the hospital on twenty-four-hour watch. I knew something like this was going to happen." He slammed his fist into the wall. Chunks of drywall fell to the floor as he withdrew his hand. "I'll fix that."

"Jacob Daniel Sanders," Sam cried from across the room.

Jacob? Mac suppressed a nervous giggle. The world was turning upside down, and she seemed to be the only person who noticed. Nate was arrested for kidnapping. Ivy was in jail for aiding and abetting a murderer. Nate going to the Feds and Ivy trying to kill herself. What next?

Jake's phone screeched. He pressed a button and read the screen aloud. "Fire at Fischer Industries."

CHAPTER 40

Jake groaned to himself. Why had he read the text aloud? Mac reacted like he'd hit her with a cattle prod.

"Let's go." She pushed past him and grabbed her coat and purse.

"We'll be right behind you." Sam closed her computer and got to her feet.

"I will stay here." Miss P remained seated. "Call if you need me to do anything."

"Do you want me to stay with you?" Sam paused, putting on her jacket.

"No, child. You go." Miss P waved a hand at her. "I'll be fine."

Mac had disappeared out the door. He found her sitting in his SUV. "Buckle up."

"Done."

They made the trip to the factory in silence except for the sirens. Fire trucks angled into the curb, and one had driven around the building via the parking lot. Dark smoke hung over the back part of the building.

"The labs." Mac ran for the front entrance.

"Hang on." Jake caught up with her. "If the fire started in the labs, we may be dealing with a chemical fire. Let's talk to the Fire Chief first." He stopped a firefighter and asked for his chief.

"He's around back."

Sam joined them and nodded at Jake and Mac.

"Is it safe to go back there?" Jake asked.

"Yes. The fire's out, and it didn't involve any toxic chemicals, but it's a good thing you guys are here. We've got a dead man."

Words no police officer wants to hear. He glanced at Mac. Her bright eyes held his for a second in unspoken fear. *Lord, please not Mr. Fischer.* He led the way to the back.

A man sat hunched on the bumper of one firetruck, his face covered by an oxygen mask. Jake unsnapped his gun. Could this be Otis Miller? As he got closer, Jake relaxed. It wasn't Miller. The man behind the mask was Mr. Fischer. Jake grinned at Mac.

But if Fischer was alive, who was dead?

"Mr. Fischer." Sam rushed to him. "We thought you were dead."

"No." The old man lowered the mask and gave them a sad smile. "But I'm sorry to say I shot Otis Miller."

Jake thrust a hand through his hair. "Please tell me it was self-defense."

"Yes. He found me in my office working." Fischer took another deep breath of oxygen. "Dragged me down to the laboratory. Tied my hands and threw me to the floor. He set fire to the place and prepared to leave." Another breath. "But in his haste, he hadn't checked my pockets, and I'd gotten in the habit of carrying a small revolver." Fischer leaned back, breathing easier now.

"I was able to shake my revolver onto the floor and grasp it with both hands while he worked. When he turned to go, I called to him. He turned, and I shot him between the eyes." One more breath of oxygen. "No one messes with my company."

"Yes, sir." Jake rubbed the bridge of his nose. The paperwork involved in this one would bury him. But at least it was self-defense. He eyed Fischer. At least he hoped so. "I need to speak to the Fire Chief."

As soon as Jake left, Mac squatted in front of Mr. Fischer. Sam perched next to him.

"How did you get to your feet?" Mac studied what she could see of his eyes above the mask.

"My legs are much improved." He avoided her gaze. "I pulled myself up on a lab stool."

"Hard to do with your hands tied."

Sam gave her a don't-be-ugly look. "I'm sure trying to escape the fire gave him the strength he needed."

Mac ignored her. "Did you pull the fire alarm?"

"The labs have an automatic alarm system." Fischer took a deep draw on the oxygen. "When I got to my feet, I staggered out of the building. The fire trucks showed up within minutes."

"Where's the gun, Mr. Fischer?"

"I dropped it in the lab." He raised defiant eyes to hers.

Nobody messed with his company.

Mac stood.

He caught her hand in his. "Thank you. For understanding."

"I'm glad you're safe." She eased her hand from his and went in search of Jake.

She was almost positive Fischer killed Otis Miller in cold blood after finding him setting fire to the labs, but she had no proof. And who's to say Miller wouldn't have tried to kill Fischer when he was discovered? He probably would have knocked Fischer out and left him to burn in the fire. If Mr. Fischer didn't have a gun.

One question nagged at her. Were Fischer's hands tied when the firefighter found him? If not, how would he explain that? A hard lump formed in her chest. She wasn't sure she could handle another person she respected and liked being put in jail.

"Yeah, I know." Jake stepped to her side as she faced the smoldering building. "A grim sight."

It took her a moment to realize he thought the bleak look on her face was meant for the view in front of her. She nodded. "What did the Fire Chief have to say?"

"An accelerant started the fire. Probably gasoline. Miller targeted files, notebooks, and any computers he could find."

"Makes sense. His goal has been to disrupt anything that could help Fischer Industries win the contract from Boeing."

"Probably manufacturing would have been his next target."

"No doubt."

"Do you think Fischer shot Miller in self-defense?" Jake rubbed the back of his neck.

Mac glanced at him. She was caught between a rock and a hard place. Jake, the detective, as well as the man she cared about, and Mr. Fischer, a good man who'd spent his whole life building a business and felt he should be able to defend it. "I don't know. But I am sure of one thing. If Miller had a chance to leave Mr. Fischer to die in the fire, he would."

"Not the same as doing it."

"No." The stone in her chest was back.

"But the law requires proof, and everything so far backs Fischer's story." Jake turned away from the damaged building. "The firefighter found him back here, wrists secured with a zip tie, breathing hard."

Mac kissed Jake on the cheek.

"What was that for?"

"For not making me ask."

A young officer jogged over. "Detective Sanders, a call came through from the Chief."

CHAPTER 41

Jake punched End and hurried around the building toward the front. "I need to get back to the precinct. Can you get a ride with Sam?"

"Of course. What's up?" Mac scrambled to keep up with him.

"Not sure." A partial truth. "Talk later." He broke into a run.

He hated leaving abruptly, but he didn't have time to tell her everything right now. When the Chief said come, he meant right then. Inside the Public Safety building, he stopped for a breath after climbing the stairs. He knocked and entered his superior's office.

"Sit, Sanders." The balding man squinted at his computer screen. "David Quinn is in custody in St. Louis. He's now Major Crimes' problem."

"I'm a member of the Major Crimes unit for St. Louis County. So ..." Jake gave his boss a quizzical look.

"I've asked for you to be excused."

Jake's expression slid into a frown. Had the Chief done so because of his niece, Ivy?

"Chief, I—"

"I know what you're thinking. It has nothing to do with Ivy or anything said about her." The older man took off his reader glasses and rubbed the bridge of his nose. "I realize I messed up. I should have had her charged right away. It might not have stopped her from trying to take her own life, but who knows? At least she would have known where she stood."

"Or it could have made things worse." An ache in the back of Jake's throat made it difficult to speak. "When someone we love is depressed, it's hard to recognize how bad it is until it's too late. Thank God someone caught her in time. All we can do now is pray Ivy realizes how many people care about her and want to see her well."

"She'll have to be charged and go to court, but I think she'll end up with a light sentence." The Chief straightened. "At least now she'll get the help she needs."

"Yes sir, and she'll have a lot of friends and family for back-up."

"Bring me up to speed on this Fischer Industries business." The Chief squared his shoulders, a signal he was ready to move on.

"The maintenance man, Otis Miller, started the fire in the labs. Fischer was in line to win a bid for a job with Boeing, and Miller's job was to sabotage the process. This fire may have accomplished that."

"I hope not. A lot of people rely on Fischer Industries for their livelihood. Including some of my own family." Chief Baker peered at Jake. "I heard how things went down out there. You're okay with his story?"

"Yes, sir." Jake shifted in his chair. "All the facts back him up."

"Good enough for me." The older man took a file from a

pile and opened it. "I've informed Homeland Security about Miller. I'll give them our final report on the matter in the morning. They may want to do their own investigation, but I doubt it. They're as eager to close the door on this one as we are."

Jake took the hint. He'd been dismissed. As he reached the door, the Chief spoke once more.

"Good to have you back, Sanders."

"Thank you, sir." Jake smiled to himself.

"And they've cleared Detective Young to return to work starting Monday. He'll be on light duty for two weeks."

"Great." Vic was coming back. Some good news for a change. But what about Claudia Smith? Would she be able to return to her job as well?

"Let me help you." Sam took hold of Mr. Fischer's arm as he prepared to rise.

"I'm fine, Mrs. Majors." The owner of Fischer Industries stood with little effort.

Sam walked beside him as he moved to a place where he could see into his ruined labs. He placed a steadying hand on the trunk of an old oak tree. His struggle to hide his pain broke her heart.

"Dad, there you are." A younger version of Fischer jogged over. "Thank God you're okay."

"I'm fine, son." The elder Fischer nodded and smiled at Sam. "Mrs. Majors has been looking after me."

"Thank you, Mrs. Majors. He's very important to us." Fischer's son took his arm. "Come home with me. We've got dinner on the table, and the extra bedroom is ready for you."

"Thank you, Mrs. Majors." Fischer reached for her hand. "We'll talk soon."

"My pleasure, Mr. Fischer." Sam waited until the pair were out of sight around the building before seeing what Fischer had put in her hand.

She held a piece of paper folded many times. As she opened it with care, she realized it was a check—a substantial check. Sam's mouth dropped open.

"Close your mouth, dear. It's very unbecoming," Mac chirped as she joined Sam.

Sam handed her the check and watched as Mac's eyes widened.

"But we didn't do anything."

"I know." Sam folded it and slid it into her pocket. "We'll have to return it."

Sam and her partner shared a moment of silence. Once again, they'd solved a case—correction, two cases—without any monetary reward.

"Have dinner with us tonight. It's been a long time, and I know Mom would love to see you." Sam took her friend's arm and started for the car.

"Thanks. I'd like that."

MAC PULLED mystery meat packages from the chest freezer. There they were—a plastic container of frozen cookies from last month. She'd take them to dinner tonight at Sam's. Replacing the meat, she put the storage container in warm water to thaw.

Thank You, Jesus. She didn't have to eat alone tonight. After Ivy and Nate and Mr. Fischer, her joy tank was running dangerously low. Her phone rang. "Hi, Jake."

"What are you doing tonight?"

"I'm going to dinner at Sam's. Why?"

"Good. I'll see you there."

"When—?" The line was dead. He'd hung up on her. Well, that was kind of rude.

CHAPTER 42

Mac parked behind Jake's SUV and carried the plate of cookies to the front door, where ferocious barking greeted her. She'd forgotten about Killer. Alan answered and clasped the dog firmly between his legs until she could enter. "My cookies and I thank you."

"No problem." He snatched one off the plate as she passed.

After depositing the plate in a safe place out of Killer's reach, she turned and greeted the wiggling dog.

"He misses you." Sam hugged her shoulders. "You need to visit more often."

"Yeah." Mac took in the room for the first time. Birthday banners hung on the mantle and over the door. Birthday?

"Happy birthday." The shout resounded in the cozy den, and Killer gave a few excited yaps.

With all that had been going on, she'd forgotten about her birthday. Her smile broadened as she realized both her sisters and their husbands were sitting on the couch, along with Miss P and Gloria Sanders.

"Say something, birthday girl." Jake put his arm around her waist.

"I didn't bring enough cookies." Her lips quivered as she fought to keep from crying.

Laughter filled the room and warmed Mac's heart.

"You brought cookies?" Jake asked.

"Yes." She elbowed him in the ribs. "You don't have to sound so amazed."

"They're actually good," Alan chimed in.

"Be nice." Sam punched him on the arm. "Dinner's ready. Do you think you can stop harassing Mac long enough to say grace?"

"Sorry." Alan grinned at his wife and bowed his head.

After a simple blessing, they filed through the kitchen, loading their plates with chicken, potato salad, green beans, carrots, and applesauce. Women first. Mac sat on a chair near her sisters.

"I can't believe you guys came all the way here for my birthday."

"Wouldn't miss it," Kate said. "But this doesn't mean you get to pass on Thanksgiving."

"Don't worry. I'll be there." Mac looked at Beth, who gave her a soft smile. They had a lot to talk about.

Jake sat on the floor by Mac. "I bet you were surprised to see your sisters here."

"I still can't believe it. How long have you guys been planning this?"

"About a month. I was afraid we were going to have to cancel when we got the call about the fire."

"You couldn't cancel," Kate said. "We were already on our way. We would have had the party without you."

"Thanks a lot," Mac said.

"Hey. You chose to be a private investigator." Her sister winked at her.

Jake touched her knee. "We're still on for tomorrow?"

Tomorrow? Three days ago, Jake asked her on a date. Tomorrow was Sunday.

"Yes." She smiled. "What time?"

"I've got a reservation for six at Marquart's Landing. I'll pick you up at twenty till."

"Fine." Something about Sunday nagged at her, and it had nothing to do with Jake. What was it?

"Time to blow out the candles, birthday girl." Sam took Mac's hand and pulled her into the kitchen.

"Before it sets off the smoke alarm," Alan said.

"Make a wish."

Mac let her gaze settle on each of her friends and family. Instead of a wish, she sent a silent prayer to heaven and blew out all the candles with one breath.

SUNDAY MORNING SUNLIGHT shone around the edges of Mac's curtains. She hopped across the cold floor and turned up the heat before diving under the covers once more.

Today would be a good day. First church, then lunch, and in the evening, her date with Jake. She sat and leaned against her headboard. Something flitted in the shadows of her memory. Something else was supposed to happen today.

She shook her herself. No sense in worrying about it. She'd have to wait for it to occur. But now it was time for a shower.

On her drive to church, something kept pushing at her consciousness. The sermon was on joy in all circumstances. Mac thrust all else aside and focused on the message.

As they left, Sam put an arm through hers. "Come to lunch with Alan, Mom, and me."

"What about Jake?"

"He's got to work, poor guy. Paperwork." Sam gave him a fake pout.

"Yeah. Go ahead. Make fun." He winked at Mac. "I'll see you later."

"You two have a date tonight?"

"Yes." Mac rolled her eyes. "And I'd love to have lunch with you."

"We thought we'd go to Colton's Steakhouse. Okay?"

"Great. Thanks for not suggesting Cowans. I love the place, but right now, it's too full of memories of Ivy."

"We figured." Alan hugged her shoulders. "We'll meet you there."

Mac hurried across the parking lot into Colton's Steakhouse. The reflection of low lights on warm wood and the rich aromas of steak and onions brought a smile to her face. Sam and Alan waved to her from a booth to her left.

"This place is making my stomach growl." She shed her coat and slid in next to Gloria Sanders.

"I hear you have a date with my son later, my dear." Gloria Sanders placed a hand on Mac's arm.

"Yes, ma'am." Warmth crept up Mac's neck to her face.

"Don't worry. I'm not about to grill you on your intentions. More like I want to commend you on your bravery."

"Bravery?" Mac raised an eyebrow at her. "I'm afraid I don't understand."

"It seems trouble is never far from him."

Mac couldn't hold a giggle. "That's what he says about me."

"Maybe you two are better suited for each other than you think."

How did Mrs. Sanders know she'd been unsure about their relationship?

The waiter came with their orders, and they reduced their comments to food. After satisfying his initial hunger, Alan took a drink.

"Yeah, Mac managed to get herself kidnapped once and almost kidnapped another time." He pointed his fork at her. "When she gets into trouble, she doesn't mess around."

The mechanical voice on the phone sprang into her mind. She stopped chewing. That was what was happening today. Robert Genovese was calling her back. But when? She dug her phone out of her purse. No calls so far.

"I remembered something." She signaled their waiter. "I'm going to need to take my food home. I'm sorry."

"What is it, Mac?" Sam asked.

"Rosa's stepfather is calling today."

CHAPTER 43

How could she have forgotten Genovese's call? Mac turned right on Highway 100. At the red caboose outside the Iron Spike Model Trains Museum, she made another right. A black truck turned behind her. She glanced in her rearview mirror. The sun reflected off the grill and blinded her.

In her mind's eye, it was night, and the truck filled her mirror. Every muscle tensed for impact. Her pulse skyrocketed, and she pressed her foot to the accelerator. At Seventh Street, she yanked the wheel left, her heart racing. Her car drifted around the corner until her back wheels caught, and she sped down the street toward home. She glanced in her mirror.

Nothing. The truck was gone. She slowed and pulled into her driveway. As she put her car in park, her daytime nightmare changed. Once again, she huddled on the floor of a big sedan, her sister screaming beside her. But this time, she heard shots.

How long had she been out? She looked at her phone. Only a few minutes. Not long enough for the neighbors to get curious and check on her. She retrieved her food bag from the floor in front of the passenger seat and went inside.

Her slaw container had opened and spilled its contents over everything in the bag. "So much for lunch." Mac tossed the whole mess in the trash and went to change clothes. Her phone vibrated in her pocket.

"Are you okay?" Jake asked.

"I'm fine." Were all the people in his family psychic?

"Sam told me you remembered about the call from Genovese at lunch. Want me to come over?"

"No." She put the phone on speaker and got out fixings for a sandwich. "If he knows about Rosa, he may not even call."

"We haven't done a deceased call yet."

"Oh." She stopped. "If he calls, should I tell him?"

"Yes. It takes away his need for you. Call me as soon as you get off the phone with him."

"Okay." She wasn't thrilled about telling the man his daughter was dead. Especially over the phone. Although it certainly would take Mac out of the equation.

She sat at the kitchen table and ate her meal.

A bang on the door woke Mac from her nap. She clambered to her feet and peeked out the front window. A police officer stood on her front porch. Had something happened to Jake? But why hadn't Sam called her?

Another bang. "Miss Love. State police. Open up."

State police? Mac unlocked the door. Two men lunged inside. One grabbed her by the arm and steered her to the couch.

"You're not police." She sprang to her feet, only to be pushed back by a hand on her chest.

A third man in a suit entered the room and took off his hat. He took a chair across from her. She met his stare with one of her own.

"You are the exact image of our Rosa." He waved a hand in front of his face. "Except for the eyes."

Mac stiffened. Robert Genovese had come in person. She had to deliver the bad news face-to-face after all. How would he take it?

"I have bad news for you."

He held up a hand. "I know. Nathanial phoned."

Of course. She studied his face. He didn't seem too upset. Maybe Nate was right not to trust him. Did he encourage David Quinn to come here and kill his daughter? But why did Nate need to tell him she was dead? And why was he here?

"I don't understand why you came. You'll need to postpone the vote until the reading of her will."

"No." He shook his impressive mane of silver hair. "No one knows she is dead except my people and yours. We can proceed with the vote and announce her death afterward."

"I've decided not to go back to Chicago with you." Mac stood, planting her feet firmly on the floor.

"That is unfortunate, but expected." He gave a slight nod to his companions.

The men moved in on her from both sides. Mac grabbed the arm of the man on her left. Putting her weight on her left leg, she side kicked the man on her right. With a loud oof, he doubled over. In a smooth motion, she brought her right knee around and jabbed the man on her left between his legs. He yelped and released her.

Genovese watched as she bested his men and ran for the front door. Mac yanked the door open. Two men, bigger than the others, stepped in and lifted her off the ground. They carried her over to the couch, where they tied her feet and hands.

"You have the same spirit as Rosa." Genovese stood. "But you are more skilled. It's time to go."

"Wait. I have a date tonight. If I don't show, he'll call out the calvary."

The silver-haired man studied her face. "Where is your phone?"

"In the kitchen. Push one."

"Remember, you will be on speaker."

Lord, I need Your help. Mac waited for Jake to answer.

"Mac, what's up?" Jake finished typing a sentence.

"I have to cancel our date tonight."

Cancel their date? They just talked about it a few hours ago. "But—"

"I've got to go out of town on business. I'll be gone a couple of days."

"What business?" The hairs on the back of his neck stood up. Something was very wrong.

"We discussed this before." She sounded angry. "Sometimes my job takes me out of town. If you can't live with that, too bad. I need to go."

Jake slammed his computer shut and grabbed his gun belt. He stopped at the front desk. "Get me back-up at Mackenzie Love's home."

CHAPTER 44

"I t's cold out there. I need to change into something warmer and use the restroom." Mac pinned Genovese with a glare.

"I will not allow you to change, but you can put a sweater or sweatshirt on over your clothes. And some heavier socks and boots." He averted his gaze. "As for the other. My man will check out the bathroom first, and he will be right outside the door at all times."

"I wouldn't expect anything else from you." Mac allowed her icy anger to surface.

Genovese snapped his eyes back to her face. A look of uncertainty settled there for a second. "Go with her to get her clothes. Undo her hands long enough for her to put them on and not a second more."

Mac needed to delay their departure as long as she could. Jake would need time to get here with help. In the bathroom, she surveyed the room for anything useful. The men had taken out everything except toilet paper, the bar of soap, and a hand towel.

And her bathrobe, still hanging on the back of the door. Had they searched the pockets? She flushed the toilet and turned on the faucet. Moving to the robe, she explored the fabric. Mac grinned as her fingers encountered a small, hard object. With slow movements, she removed the nail clippers from the bathrobe and dropped it into her pants pocket. One for her. She washed and dried her hands. It wouldn't do for the soap to be dry.

In her bedroom, one man took off her zip ties. She pulled a sweater over her head. As soon as it settled on her torso, he grabbed her hands and placed a new tie on them.

"Where are your socks?"

"I'll get them."

"No. I'll do it."

Mac showed him and indicated what boots she wanted. They tugged her down the hall to the living room, where Genovese waited.

"I'm going to need help with my socks and boots."

"Help her." The boss man lifted his chin at his henchmen.

"We didn't sign up as babysitters," one man grumbled.

"I pay you enough to do whatever I ask."

He got down on one knee and laid his gun on the floor. "Give me your socks."

"I hear sirens. Hurry." The other man strode to the front window. "They're coming this way."

Genovese narrowed his eyes at Mac. "What did you do?"

She drove her knees into the face of the man kneeling before her. He grunted and lost his balance, falling to one side. Mac dove for the floor as the man at the window turned and shot.

"No." Genovese yelled. "I need her alive."

"Sorry." The man turned back to the window. "False alarm. They passed by."

"Let's hope the neighbors didn't hear the shot, you idiot." Genovese stood. "No more delays. Put her boots on and let's go."

Mac fought as best she could, but it was no use. The men were too much for her, with her legs and arms tied. At the car, they hesitated.

"It's risky having her up front with us, boss."

"Yeah. You saw what she can do."

"I'm afraid you're right." Genovese touched her cheek. "I'm sorry, my dear."

The head thug pressed a button, and the trunk lid popped up.

"No." Mac threw herself against her capturers. "Don't put me in the trunk."

They lifted her, tossed her inside, and slammed the lid.

Something inside warned Jake to survey the situation at Mackenzie's house before going in gun drawn. And he was glad he did. He eased to the curb and pulled his binoculars from the console. Two black luxury sedans sat in her driveway. Nose to trunk.

As he watched, two men came out of the house, one with a pained look on his face. They got in the car closest to the street. Sirens broke the silence of the quiet neighborhood, and Jake lifted his radio to his lips.

"Pass by the house. Go around the block and turn off your lights and sirens. Park on High Street and wait for my signal."

The squad cars screamed past him and turned the corner onto Klingslick Lane. He ducked down and prayed he was handling this correctly, and that Mac didn't get hurt in the process.

Her door opened once more, and two more thugs carried Mac to the car in back. A fifth man came out and closed the door. The leader of the group. After a brief discussion, the trunk lid lifted. "No." A hard fist of fear squeezed his heart. The lid closed, and his fear morphed into stone cold rage. He keyed his police radio. "Move in. Be advised. Mac is in the trunk of one of the cars."

Doors slammed shut, and they gunned out of the driveway, headed away from Jake. He sped after them, lights and sirens blaring. Two police cars sat side-by-side, blocking the street at the corner of High. The men had nowhere to go. *Please, Lord, let them give up without a fight.*

The drivers emerged from behind tinted windows with hands in the air.

"Tell all your passengers to exit the vehicle with hands raised." Jake trained his pistol on the driver of the second car. "You. Back up toward me."

The man did as he was told.

"Open the trunk."

The lid swung up, revealing Mac laying on her left side.

"It's about time." She glared at him.

Relief flooded through him. She was good. "Okay. You can shut it again."

The man's eyes widened.

"No, Jake. Please. I didn't mean it."

"Just kidding." He motioned with his pistol. "Take off her restraints and help her out of there."

"Do I have to? I've seen what she can do."

"So have I." Jake grinned. "I suggest you be nice and apologize."

The man clipped her ties and lifted her out of the trunk. "Sorry, miss."

"Uh huh." Mac rubbed her wrists and joined Jake. "Robert Genovese is in one of these cars. He came in person instead of calling."

"That's not Mr. Genovese," the driver said.

CHAPTER 45

But he had to be Robert Genovese. He'd told her he was. Hadn't he? Mac stared at the man standing before them. "If he's not Genovese, who is he?"

"Luigi Bono, his ... consigliere." The man shrugged. "Kind of an advisor, but more."

"Like in the Godfather?"

"Yes."

Mac shared a look with Jake.

"Whatever he is, he's being arrested for attempted kidnapping, along with the rest of your crew. Turn around and put your hands behind your back." Jake pulled a pair of handcuffs off his belt.

Mac rubbed her wrists again as she ran through the conversations between her and the silver-haired man. She assumed he was Genovese, and he let her believe it. Did his employer even know Bono was here?

"Jake, if I were you, I'd call Genovese to see if he's aware of what his trusted advisor has been up to."

"Good idea." He motioned to one of his officers to take the driver away. "I'll need to interview Luigi Bono tonight."

They walked back to her house.

"Yes." She sighed. Another date interrupted. This one with a sumptuous dinner promised. Her stomach growled.

"I'm sorry." Jake pulled her into his arms. "If I hadn't been such an idiot, we could have had two or three dates by now."

"That's okay. I'm not sure I was ready either." She settled against his chest and stored away the feeling of warmth and the sound of his heartbeat for her dreams.

"Are you sure you're ready now?" He lifted her face and pressed his lips to hers.

Another kind of warmth spread through her, and she returned his kiss. After a while, she leaned back. "Not fair. Now you're going to work and leave me."

"I can come back later."

"I don't think that's a good idea." She disengaged herself from him. He gave her the look again—and she almost changed her mind. "But I would like to know how the interview goes."

"You're right. A call would be better." He brushed her cheek with a kiss and opened the door for her. "Sweet dreams."

As she stood by the window and watched Jake leave, she knew her dreams would be sweet indeed. The question was, did her feelings for him go beyond the stuff of dreams?

Maybe it was time to figure out once and for all what she felt for her best friend's brother. But how? She had no mother to talk to, but she had her sisters. Yet another subject to discuss with them at Thanksgiving. It was going to be a busy holiday visit. Mac pulled up her calendar. She left for Kansas City on Wednesday. In three days.

She should start packing. The weather was the same as Washington—cold. She wandered back to her bedroom and began rummaging through her closet. But she found it hard to keep her mind on preparing for her trip.

What if Robert Genovese knew nothing about Dr. David Quinn? What if this had been Luigi Bono all along? He passed himself off as Genovese to her. Why not to Quinn? She should be at the precinct. She threw the sweater she was holding on her bed and marched out of her bedroom.

Halfway down the hall, she stopped. No. Jake was a good detective. She needed to let him do his job. She spun around and stomped back into the bedroom. An hour later, she was packed except for last-minute things like her electric toothbrush and make-up. Her stomach growled.

In the kitchen, her phone showed a missed call from Jake. She pressed one and plopped into a chair.

"Where've you been?"

"Packing. I forgot to bring my phone into the bedroom."

"I thought you weren't leaving until Wednesday."

"I needed something to do. Jake, come on. What did you find out?"

"You had a good idea. I called Genovese. He didn't know Bono was here or that his stepdaughter was dead."

"I knew it." Mac struggled between feeling exhilarated at being right and sympathetic for the Chicago businessman. "Did you ask him about Dr. Quinn?"

"I did. He never heard of him." A note of satisfaction sounded in Jake's voice. "I'm guessing Bono tricked him like he tricked you."

A frisson of excitement passed through Mac. Right again. Although she wasn't too sure she liked the being tricked part. More like misled.

"Bono finally caved and told us he'd planned to get Rosa's shares and eventually wrest control of the company from Genovese. His words, not mine."

A kernel of sadness lodged in Mac's throat. "Do you think Nate knew what Bono was up to?"

"I don't know. I'll turn all this over to the Feds. They'll have to figure that one out."

"I guess that's it then." No case meant no reason to see Jake daily. The kernel of sadness grew into a lump.

"Yep. All done except the paperwork." A pause. "I'll need you to come in sometime and give a statement before you leave."

"I can come tomorrow." Her spirits rose.

"Late morning. Maybe we could swing lunch."

"I'd like that." The corners of her mouth lifted in a smile.

JAKE UNLOCKED his door and threw his keys on the table in the small foyer. The aroma from the paper bag in his hand had his salivary glands working overtime. He was so hungry he would consider eating sushi—and he hated sushi. Lucky for him, he wouldn't have to.

The first bite of a good burger is always the best, and he savored it. As he prepared to stuff a half dozen fries into his mouth, a strange mewing sound came from the back of the house.

"Duchess? Are you all right?" He got to his feet and headed down the hall toward the bedrooms, turning on lights as he went. "Duchess?"

Why had he let her go outside? The mewing grew louder as he approached his bedroom. Flecks of mud and grass trailed down the hall. Was that blood? He knew this would happen. She had gotten into a fight and dragged herself home where she lay mangled and dying, waiting for his return.

"I'm here, sweetheart." He flipped the overhead light on in

his bedroom and stopped dead. A calm Duchess lay on a discarded bath towel nursing four tiny mewing babies. She raised her head and regarded him with those brilliant emerald green eyes.

"I'll leave you to it." Jake smiled at her, turned out the light, and returned to his meal.

CHAPTER 46

Sam lifted the heavy pan from the oven and placed it on the stove out of Killer's reach. Anyone entering her house would recognize the bouquet of smells as a traditional Thanksgiving dinner—from the turkey to pumpkin pie. The only thing marring the day was that her father couldn't be there.

"Killer. Back up. You'll burn your nose." She closed the oven. Her sweet dog kept looking at her with those big brown eyes, pleading for a bite. "Sorry. This is people food. You get yummy dog food."

The goldendoodle sighed and padded out of the room.

"Do I get people food?" Alan slid his arms around her.

"Only if you're good."

He nuzzled her neck. "Is this good?"

"Yes, but not right now. I've got to get the food on the table. You can help."

He disengaged and held out his hands. "Gladly. I think we're all starved."

"I need you to carve the turkey." She picked up a bowl of mashed potatoes. "I'll get Jake to help."

After a few trips, Sam took off her apron. "We're ready. Alan, would you say grace?"

While listening to her husband's simple yet sincere prayer, Sam's own heart swelled with thanks for all the beautiful blessings in her life. Family and friends, good health, and many more.

"Beautiful prayer as usual," Gloria Sanders said, as she reached for the cranberry sauce. "And the food looks amazing. Where is Mackenzie today?"

"I asked her to come, but she's spending Thanksgiving with her sisters in Kansas City." Sam offered her a roll. "Miss P is with family in St. Louis."

"Oh good. I do hate for friends to be alone on holidays."

"Me too." Sam couldn't imagine anything worse. Thank God for Alan. And Jake and her mom. "Speaking of which." She cut a look at her brother. "I heard you and Mac had lunch on Monday."

He swallowed. "We did."

"And?"

"And." He laid his hands, clutching his knife and fork, on the table to either side of his plate. "We've decided to start seriously dating. Whatever that means."

"Congratulations." Alan chuckled. "The first step."

"To what?"

"To marriage."

Jake blanched. "We're taking it very slow."

"Of course you are."

Gloria Sanders cleared her throat. "May I change the subject?"

"Please do." Jake looked like he could have kissed her.

"I was wondering what you could tell us about the reading of Miss Lombardi's will yesterday."

Everyone stopped eating. Jake finished chewing and swallowed. What could he tell them? "I guess it's a matter of public record now."

"Who was there?"

"Mr. Fischer, myself, and a couple of representatives from the company. Mac had already left for Kansas City."

"What did it say? Who did she leave her shares to?" Alan asked.

"First, the lawyer read a letter written to Rosa by her mother." Jake raised a hand to stop any protests. "You need to know about it in order to understand the rest. Rosa's mother gave her advice on who to leave her inheritance to when it came time."

"She wished the company to remain in the family, no doubt," Gloria said.

"And the majority stockholders to be women. Rosa's mother grew up with a cousin that was more like a sister. She lost track of her, but knew her cousin had at least two daughters. In her letter to Rosa, she advised her to leave her inheritance to her female second cousins—if she didn't have a daughter of her own by then."

"Did Rosa take her advice?"

"Yes. She left her inheritance to the female heirs of her mother's cousin. Mr. Fischer's son, Brandon, is her executor. He has two years to find Rosa's second cousins and distribute her inheritance among them."

"What was her mother's cousin's name?"

"Marie Rialto."

"I know Rosa owned majority stock in the business, but how much money are we talking?" Alan asked.

"Don't be so crude." Sam slapped him on the arm.

"It's okay. We're all wondering the same thing." Jake laughed. "All I know for sure is Rosa's dividends last year totaled three hundred thousand dollars."

Alan whistled.

"Some young women are about to get news that will change their lives forever," Gloria Sanders said. "For good or for bad."

"What if he can't find the women?" Sam asked.

"The instructions are to research women entrepreneurs and find one worthy of Rosa's inheritance."

"I'm glad I'm not Brandon Fischer," Alan said.

"You and me both." Jake gave a mirthless laugh.

THANKSGIVING DAY with her sisters was all Mac had hoped it would be. Good food, fellowship, and lots of fun. She'd caught them up on what had been happening. They shared her grief over Ivy and helped her hash out her relationship with Jake. With their help, she decided on a course of action—to enjoy his company and stop analyzing her feelings. And she still had another two days to go.

Mac settled into the large armchair by the fire. The time with her sisters and their families mended all the rips in her soul. Was she ready to tear a new hole with her questions? But if she didn't, she was positive the visions would turn into nightmares.

"I know what you're thinking." Beth sipped her hot chocolate. "It's not a question of being ready. Your mind is telling you it's time, or you wouldn't be having those episodes."

"You're right." Mac placed her mug on the table beside her. "Tell me what they're about."

"When you were a toddler—two or three years old—we lived in New York City."

"New York? All the stories about our German ancestors were lies?"

"Mac, there's a lot you don't know. Please listen."

"Okay." How could she forget living in New York?

"What you're seeing in your visions is one night in December when we all piled into the car to go look at the Christmas lights downtown and the store windows. We did that every year. It was so beautiful." Beth's eyes unfocused at the memory before turning grim. "But this year, something awful happened. Some men in a car coming from the other way stuck big guns out the window and shot up the car in front of us."

The gun shots she heard in her last episode. "Is that why you screamed?"

"Yes. Me and Kate both. I pushed you onto the floor behind mother's seat. Daddy swerved the car into the curb and slammed on the brakes. He kept yelling for us to stay down."

"Is that why we left New York?"

"In a way." Beth picked at the afghan next to her on the couch. "Daddy saw the whole thing, and he offered to be a witness."

Mac stiffened. "Was it a mob hit?"

"Yes."

"And Daddy volunteered to be a witness against the mob?" She was on the edge of her chair now.

Beth nodded, tears in her eyes. "You can probably guess the rest. We were put in witness protection, given new names, and relocated to Washington, Missouri."

"Please tell me Mom and Dad's accident when we were older was truly an accident." But Mac knew the answer before her sister uttered a word.

"The mob never forgets nor forgives. The part you never knew about their accident—the part no one ever knew except me and the police—was Dad was shot through the forehead before he lost control of the car." Beth held out her arms. "I'm so sorry. I should have told you a long time ago, but I ... you know how hard it was on me."

Mac curled on the sofa next to her big sister. All her sister had said tumbled around in her brain like giant boulders, knocking down all the structures of her life. Her parents were murdered. What were their real names? Did Chief Baker know about what had happened? Did Jake?

"What was my real name?" Mac closed her eyes.

"Do you really want to know?"

Did she? "Yes."

"Elizabeth Rialto."

The End

AUTHOR'S NOTE

The Case of Mistaken Identity is my second book set in Washington, Missouri. Since finishing my first, I've had a chance to spend more time in this great town set on the Missouri River. When we lived in St. Louis, our visits were for fun, but now I come for business and pleasure.

This past visit, I got to spend time with Detective Lieutenant Steve Sitzes in his office at the police station, eat at a few more restaurants, and I had a book signing at Neighborhood Reads Bookstore. It was a wonderful trip!

The problem with writing about a real town is that an author can make mistakes, and I made two that I know of in my first book. So I'd like to take this opportunity to apologize.

The first one was not a big one, but I will not repeat it. I had a freight train blowing a crossing signal at the Lafayette Street crossing. I realized on my second research visit that trains aren't allowed to do that. Oops. No more crossing signal whistles will be blown in my books.

The second that I've found was big, and I have no excuse except that I did not do my homework. I had the Missouri

Meerschaum Pipe factory being converted to condos! Which is not true!

The Missouri Meerschaum Company got its beginning with a Dutch immigrant named Henry Tibbe. He began making corn cob pipes as early as 1869, and by 1907 the Missouri Meerschaum Company was established.

Today, Washington, Missouri, is known as the "Corn Cob Pipe Capital of the World" and the Missouri Meerschaum Company is going strong. There is a museum on the corner of the building where you can learn about the history of the company and purchase your own corn cob pipe and accessories.

I apologize to the Missouri Meerschaum Corn Cob Pipe Company, the city of Washington, and to my readers for making such an error.

I'm sure there are other mistakes I've made, and for those I also beg your forgiveness. More than likely, I made a few more in this book as well. It's very hard to produce a good story and get things right without living in a place. I get home from a research trip and think of a thousand things I should have done while I was there. Well, maybe not a thousand, but at least ten.

I can only pray that my mistakes do not take away from your enjoyment of my story, and that I haven't caused any hard feelings in anyway. If so, please let me know.

You can reach me at dsprink2@gmail.com

Thank you for sharing your town with me.

ABOUT THE AUTHOR

When Deborah Sprinkle retired, she had a plan for keeping busy. Part of that plan was to write a mystery novel.

After collaborating with Kendra Armstrong on her non-fiction book entitled *Exploring the Faith of America's Presidents*, Deborah turned her hand to fiction.

It took several years of honing her craft before Deborah realized her dream. Deadly Guardian debuted in May 2019, with Mantle Rock Publishing. Deborah's second book in the series, *Death of an Imposter*, came out November 24, 2020, and the third, *Silence Can Be Deadly*, November 2, 2021, both with Scrivenings Press.

Her new series debuted in 2022, with *The Case of the*

Innocent Husband. She also had a novella published that year and a short story in an anthology. Deborah continued to win awards for her short stories, articles, and flash fiction.

Deborah lives in Memphis with her greatest fan, her husband of 50+ years, and describes herself as an ordinary woman serving an extraordinary God.

The Case of the Innocent Husband

by Deborah Sprinkle

A Mac & Sam Mystery - Book One

Private Investigator Mackenzie Love needs to do one thing. Find out who shot Eleanor Davis. Or she'll have to leave town.

When Eleanor Davis is found shot in her garage, the only suspect, her estranged husband, is found not guilty in a court of law. However, most of the good citizens of Washington, Missouri, remain unconvinced. It doesn't matter that twelve men and women of the jury found him not guilty. What do they know?

And since Private Investigator Mackenzie Love accepted the job for the defense and helped acquit Connor Davis, her friends and neighbors have placed her squarely in the enemy camp. Therefore, her overwhelming goal becomes to find out who killed Eleanor Davis.

Or leave the town she grew up in.

As the investigation progresses, the threats escalate. Someone wants to stop Mackenzie and her partner, Samantha Majors, and is willing to do whatever it takes—including murder.

Can Mac and Sam find the killer before they each end up on the wrong side of a bullet?

Get your copy here:

https://scrivenings.link/innocenthusband

Silence Can Be Deadly

Trouble in Pleasant Valley

Book Three

It started with a taxi ride ... or did it?

Forced from the career he loved and into driving a taxi, Peter Grace had grown accustomed to his simple life. Until one night when a suspicious fare and a traffic jam blew it all apart, and he was on the run again. Only this time it wasn't a matter of changing occupations but of life and death.

He needed help and he knew where to find it. His old friend Rafe in Pleasant Valley. What he didn't count on was finding not only the help he needed but a community of new friends and the love of his life. Zoe Poole.

The story of Captain Nate Zuberi and his wife Madison continues as they too risk their lives to help Peter. Along with Peter, Rafe, and Zoe, they strive to catch an assassin.

But can the group of friends find the killer before anyone else gets hurt?

Death of an Imposter

Trouble in Pleasant Valley

Book Two

Her first week on the job and rookie detective Bernadette Santos has been given the murder of a prominent citizen to solve. But when her victim turns out to be an imposter, her straight forward case takes a nasty turn. One that involves the attractive Dr. Daniel O'Leary, a visitor to Pleasant Valley and a man harboring secrets.

When Dr. O'Leary becomes a target of violence himself, Detective Santos has two mysteries to unravel. Are they related? And how far can she trust the good doctor? Her heart tugs her one way while her mind pulls her another. She must discover the solutions before it's too late!

Deadly Guardian

Trouble in Pleasant Valley

Book One

Madison Long, a high school chemistry teacher, looks forward to a relaxing summer break. Instead, she suffers through a nightmare of threats, terror, and death. When she finds a man murdered she once dated, Detective Nate Zuberi is assigned to the case, and in the midst of chaos, attraction blossoms into love.

Together, she and Nate search for her deadly guardian before he decides the only way to truly save her from what he considers a hurtful relationship is to kill her—and her policeman boyfriend as well.

Sharktooth Island

A collection of Romantic Suspense novellas

A fabled island that no one dares to tame.

This collection contains four novellas:

Book 1 - Out of the Storm *(1830)* by Susan Page Davis

Laura Bryant sails with her father and his three-man crew on his small coastal trading schooner. After a short stay in Jamaica, where she meets Alex Dryden, an officer on another ship, the Bryants set out for their home in New England.

In a storm, they are blown off course east of Savannah, Georgia, to a foreboding island. Captain Bryant tells his daughter he's heard tales of that isle. It's impossible to land on, though it looks green and inviting from a distance. It has no harbor but is surrounded by dangerous rocks and cliffs.

Pirates outrun the storm and decide to bury a cache of treasure on this island and return for it later. On board is Alex, whom the cutthroats captured in Jamaica and forced to work for them. Alex risks his own life to escape the pirates and tries to help Laura and Captain Bryant outwit them. Beneath the deadly struggle, romance blossoms for Laura.

Book 2 - *A Passage of Chance* (1893) by Linda Fulkerson

Orphaned at a young age, Melody Lampert longs to escape the loveless home of the grandmother who begrudgingly raised her. Stripped of her inheritance due to her grandmother's resentments, Melody discovers her name remains on the deed of one property—an obscure island off the Georgia coast that she shares with her cousin. But when he learns the island may contain a hidden pirate treasure, he's determined to cheat her out of her share.

Ship's mechanic Padric Murphy made a vow to his dying father— break the curse that has plagued their family for generations. To do so, he must return what was taken from Sharktooth Island decades earlier—a pair of rare gold pieces. His opportunity to right the wrong arrives when his new employer sets sail to explore the island.

After a series of unexplainable mishaps occur, endangering Padric and his boss's beautiful cousin Melody, he fears his chance of breaking the curse may be ruined. But is the island's greed thwarting his plans? Or the greed of someone else?

Book 3 - *Island Mayhem* (1937) by Elena Hill

Louise Krause stopped piloting to pursue nursing, but when money got too tight she was forced to give up her dreams and start ferrying around a playboy who managed to excel during the Great Depression. When a routine aerial tour turns south, Louise is unable to save the plane.

After crash landing, the cocky pilot is stranded. She longs to escape the uninhabited island, but her makeshift raft sinks, and she and her companions are in even worse trouble. Can Louise learn to trust the others in order to survive, or will the island's curse and potential sabotage lead to her demise?

Book 4 - *After the Storm* (*present day*) by Deborah Sprinkle

Mercedes Baxter inherited two passions from her father—a love for Sharktooth Island, a spit of land in the middle of the ocean left to her in his will, and a dedication to the study of the flora and fauna on and around its rocky landscape.

For the last five years, since graduating from college, Mercy led a peaceful, simple life on the island with only her cat, Hawkeye, for company. Through grant money she obtained from a conservancy in Savannah, she could live on her island while studying and writing about the plants and animals there. Life was perfect.

But when a hurricane hits the island, Mercy's life changes for good. Her high school sweetheart, Liam Stewart, shows up to help her with repairs, and ignites the flame that has never quite died away. And if that's not enough, while assessing the damage to the island, they make a discovery that puts both their lives in danger.

Stay up-to-date on your favorite books and authors with our free e-newsletters.

ScriveningsPress.com